ANASTASIA
AGAIN!

ANASTASIA AGAIN!

Lois Lowry

Decorations by Diane deGroat

A YEARLING BOOK

Published by
Bantam Doubleday Dell Books for Young Readers
a division of
Bantam Doubleday Dell Publishing Group, Inc.
1540 Broadway
New York, New York 10036

ISBN: 0-440-40009-0

Reprinted by arrangement with Houghton Mifflin Company

Printed in the United States of America

One Previous Edition

August 1992

26   25   24   23   22

OPM

To Laura Beard

ANASTASIA AGAIN!

1

"The suburbs!" said Anastasia. "We're moving to the *suburbs?* I can't believe it. I can't believe that you would actually do such a thing to me. I'm going to kill myself. As soon as I finish this chocolate pudding, I'm going to jump out the window."

"We live on the first floor," her mother reminded her. "You've been jumping out of your window for years. The first time you jumped out of your window was when you were three years old and didn't want to take a nap any more."

"Yeah," said Anastasia, remembering. "You thought I'd been kidnapped, when you came to my room to wake me up and I was gone. Actually I was outside picking all your tulips."

"I could have killed you for that. It was the first time I'd ever grown really terrific tulips."

"I wish you *had* killed me for that. Because there isn't any point in living if you have to live in the suburbs."

Her father put down the magazine he was reading, *The New York Review of Books.* He was reading an article called "Morality and Mythology." Anastasia didn't have any idea what that meant; but she liked it that her father knew what it meant and that he liked reading about it, and she was absolutely certain that there wasn't a single person in the entire suburbs of the United States who would ever in his entire life read an article called "Morality and Mythology."

"How on earth," asked her father, "can you be so sure you would hate the suburbs when you have never lived anyplace but this apartment?"

"Daddy," Anastasia pointed out. "I *read.* You know that. You yourself taught me to read when I was four years old. I read books about the suburbs. I know what people who live there are like."

"Oh? And what are they like?"

"Not like us, that's for sure. One, they live in split-level houses with sets of matching furniture. Can you *imagine* that? Rooms of cute matching furniture? Good grief. I mean, think for a minute about our living room here in this apartment. Think of all the neat stuff we have in it."

They thought. "Books," said her mother.

"Right. Millions of books. There aren't any bookcases in split-level houses. Right where the bookcases should be, people in the suburbs have a huge color TV instead."

"We have a TV," said her father. "In fact, I'm about to miss the first inning of the Red Sox game."

"Daddy, we have an ancient, small black-and-white TV. And there are books on top of it, books behind it, books in front of it. That's not the same. I'm talking about a monster color TV, and on top of it is a bowl of fake fruit."

"Fake fruit? Are you sure of that, Anastasia?"

"Absolutely. Just look in the Sears ads in the paper. But forget that for a minute. Think some more about our own living room."

"Paintings," said her mother. "I think people in the suburbs have paintings on their walls."

"Wrong," said Anastasia. "The paintings on our walls are real. We have some of your paintings, Mom. And we have that one that I did of a rooster, when I was five. And we have that really neat one by your friend Annie, Dad . . ."

"I wish you'd get rid of that, Myron," said Anastasia's mother.

"Annie was a fine painter," muttered her father. "And a fine person. You would have liked her. You will like her if she ever comes back from Central America. We'll have her for dinner."

"Over my dead body we'll have her for dinner," said Anastasia's mother.

"Mom. Daddy. You're missing the point. The point is that we have meaningful paintings on our walls."

"And people in the suburbs do not?"

"No, they definitely don't. They have pictures of the

Sierra Nevadas, painted-by-number. Or else pictures of kittens with big eyes, playing with balls of yarn. It goes with the matched set of furniture."

"Actually," said her mother, "our furniture is pretty awful, some of it."

"No, it isn't! We're the only people in the whole world who have a white couch with a big sunflower embroidered on it!"

"Anastasia, the only reason for the sunflower is because I had to do something to cover up the spot where Sam threw up."

"But that's okay! I mean it's okay in the *city*. But if we lived in a split-level house in some development, people wouldn't understand it."

"ANASTASIA," said her father, in the booming voice that he used only when he was beginning to be quite annoyed with something, "YOU'RE MAKING ASSUMPTIONS."

"I am not. I never make anything. I didn't make the school basketball team, even."

"You are making assumptions."

"I don't even know what assumptions are. I can't even make decent brownies."

"*Premature* assumptions!"

"I didn't make the finals in the sixth-grade spelling bee. I can't make *anything*."

"YOU ARE MAKING HASTY JUDGMENTS! IDIOTIC PREMATURE ASSUMPTIONS! AND YOU ARE ALSO MAKING ME MISS THE RED SOX GAME ON TV!"

Now Anastasia knew that he was really getting mad.

She scowled. "I hardly ever even make my bed," she muttered. "The last thing I ever made in my life was a dumb potholder, in third grade. I *never* made a premature assumption. If I did, it would come out crooked."

Her mother sighed. "I'll tell you what you make, Anastasia. You make life very difficult sometimes." She began to pick up the chocolate pudding bowls from the table. "Let's let your dad watch the ball game. I'm going to wash these dishes. You want to help, or do you want to get Sam up from his nap? We can talk about all of this later."

"I'll go get Sam. Unless maybe he's already jumped out the window. He's getting old enough to figure stuff like that out."

She wandered down the hallway of the apartment, thumping the walls as she went. It made a nice, hollow, echoing sound in the dark hall. Anastasia had noticed that for the first time when she was three or four and had been thumping the walls ever since. There were handprints way down low, from when she was very small; handprints higher up, from when she was bigger (and a dark stain at that height: she had squashed a tomato there when she was nine and very angry about something); and now that she was twelve and beginning to be quite tall, her handprints were appearing at a level that had never had handprints before.

The whole apartment had a history, and it was *her* history and her parents' history and beginning to be Sam's.

She had planned to show Sam how to thump the walls with that hollow sound very soon. The thought of moving made her stomach ache.

"And we didn't even have a chance to talk about the *other* stuff!" she called back toward the kitchen, where she could hear her mother washing the dishes. "That we would have to have a *car,* for pete's sake! We would have to pollute the atmosphere with a car! And I would have to do dumb suburban stuff. Probably I would have to be a Girl Scout!"

There wasn't any answer from her mother. In the living room, she could hear her father turn the volume up on the TV to drown her out.

"You could never *ever* wear jeans any more, you know, Mom!" she called. "Ladies in the suburbs only wear cute cotton dresses from Lord and Taylor's!"

No answer. She stood still for a minute outside Sam's door.

"And they play *bridge* every afternoon! And have affairs with the neighbors' husbands! Do you *realize* that?"

No answer. Her mother was washing the dishes very loudly, which meant that she was getting pretty mad. In a minute she would probably throw a dish.

"Oh, rats," muttered Anastasia to herself, and opened the door to her brother's room. Once, before Sam was born, it had been the dining room. It was true that they were outgrowing the apartment. But it didn't matter. Not as much as the other things mattered.

"Hi, Sam," said Anastasia. Her brother was sitting in his crib with a blanket over his head, chuckling. "Quit being so cute," she said. "I have terrible news." Sam took the blanket off his head and looked at her. His face had sleeping wrinkles on it.

"Frank Goldfish is going to die," said Anastasia sorrowfully. "Goldfish can't survive things like moving to the suburbs. Suburban goldfish are different, anyway. They have tanks with all that plastic junk in them: castles and little fake divers. Frank just likes his little ordinary city-goldfish bowl. I am quite certain that Frank will not survive this."

Then she realized that Sam didn't care about that. It was Sam who had flushed Frank the First down the toilet.

"And also," she told him sadly, "I know that your blanky won't survive. Moving men absolutely refuse to move grubby old blankies. I'm sorry to tell you that, Sam." She lifted him out of his crib and took his faded yellow blanket away from him. He grabbed for it, missed, and burst into howls.

"It's really too bad about your blanky, Sam," Anastasia said in a soft, mournful voice. "I suppose we'll have to put it out for the trash men to pick up."

Sam stamped his small bare feet. "Gimme my blanky!" he roared, grabbing for it. Anastasia held it up higher.

"I'm so terribly sorry, Sam," she said in a stricken tone that she was imitating from an old movie that had been rerun on TV recently. George Brent telling Bette Davis that she had a brain tumor.

Sam's howls turned into shrieks, and he threw himself on the floor and began to kick.

"Mom? Dad?" called Anastasia. "I just told Sam the news! Can you hear him? He doesn't want to move to the suburbs either!"

❖

Anastasia went to her room to sulk. She always left the door open when she was sulking. She had perfected the art of sulking, and one of the essential points was that people had to *know* you were doing it. So it was important to leave the door open.

She lay on her bed, which was the best place for sulking, and was visible from her open door. But when no one was walking past her room, sulking was boring. So, to pass the time, she got out the notebook in which she intended to write a mystery novel. She had been intending to write it for almost a year, as soon as she could think of a title. She had decided to write a mystery after she began to think that Nancy Drew mysteries had no relationship to real life. Whose real life, after all, included haunted houses, spiral staircases, or twisted candlesticks? Yet real life — especially Anastasia's real life — was full of mysteries. For almost a year, she had been making notes about the mysteries of her own existence. None of them yet seemed to lend themselves to an entire book. "The Mystery of Why I Am Not Allowed to Go to X-rated Movies Even Though I Have Known All the Facts of Life Since I Was Six," for example, was a legitimate mystery of real life; but she couldn't seem to go on to write a novel about it.

Now, angrily, she wrote, "The Mystery of Why Some

People Make Decisions without Consulting Their Twelve-Year-Old Children." Then she wrote, "Chapter One: Decisions about Moving to the (Ugh) Suburbs."

But she got so mad, just thinking about it, that she didn't write anything else. It was hard to write in a notebook while you were lying on a bed anyway. It was much easier just to lie back and sulk.

2

"Daddy?" asked Anastasia, as she stood in the bathroom door that evening, watching her father give Sam a bath. "Have you and Mom ever given serious thought to what a weird baby Sam is?"

It was true, what she said. Right now, for example, Sam was sitting in the bathtub, and he looked like any ordinary two-and-a-half-year-old baby. He had a fat stomach with a poking-out bellybutton, rosy cheeks, curly brown hair, brown eyes with long eyelashes, and he had soapsuds in his ears, which was kind of cute. A minute ago he had squirmed and wiggled and screeched when his father had washed his face, which was an ordinary two-and-a-half-year-old baby thing to do.

But then he had said firmly and with dignity, "Don't

get soap in my eyes, please. My eyes are very sensitive."

That was weird. The little boy next door could only say things like ma-ma, da-da, by-by, and ordinary baby things.

Sam had *never* said ma-ma or da-da or by-by. He had started talking like Walter Cronkite before he was a year old. Anastasia's mother *swore* that one day when he was four months old, he had said, "Thank you," when she fed him some strained apricots; but no one believed her, and she had no witnesses.

"He's not weird," said Anastasia's father, lifting Sam out of the tub. "It's just that people develop at different rates. For example, Anastasia, you are twelve years old, but you are already five feet seven inches tall . . ."

"I *know* that, Daddy. You don't really need to *remind* me of that, Daddy."

"I only bring it up because it is an unusual height for a twelve-year-old girl. You've grown fast, height-wise. But at the same time, your body is still quite straight, up and down. I mean, you haven't yet begun to mature much physically, except for height. You don't yet have *hips*, for example, or . . ."

"Daddy. Don't be gross."

"There's nothing gross about hips. I was just pointing out that different aspects of people develop at different rates. Now in many ways, Sam is still a baby. Cut that out, Sam."

Sam was eating toothpaste.

"I like it," said Sam. "I like the flavor."

"Well, it costs a dollar fifty-nine a tube. Cut it out."

He began to dry Sam with a big blue towel.

"See what I mean, Anastasia? He's mischievous, like all toddlers. And he still wears diapers because he hasn't achieved the physical maturity to be toilet trained. I *wish* you would be toilet trained, Sam."

"No," said Sam, and smiled sweetly.

"And he still has his security blanket, like many babies . . ."

"Where is my blanky?" asked Sam. "I want it right now."

"Mom washed it while you were having your bath," said Anastasia. "It's in the dryer."

"Well, I want it when I go to bed," said Sam firmly.

Dr. Krupnik pinned on Sam's diapers and snapped up his pajamas.

"There you are, old buddy. Go find your mom."

Sam padded off down the hall.

"It's just that he is verbally precocious," said Anastasia's father, leaning over to scrub out the tub. "He's unusual, that way. But I wouldn't call him — what did you call him? — a weird baby."

"Well, okay then, he's unusual. Don't you and Mom realize what a *disaster* it would be to move an unusual baby like Sam to the suburbs? In the suburbs all babies are alike."

"You're sure of that?"

"Absolutely. All suburban babies ride around in shopping carts at supermarkets, and whine, and their mothers slap them."

"Their mothers *slap* them?"

"Absolutely. Their mothers all have pink curlers in their hair. Do you want that to happen to Mom, and to Sam?"

Dr. Krupnik sighed. "Anastasia, get me a beer from the refrigerator. As soon as your mom puts Sam to bed, we will talk some more about this move which we are going to make."

"Did I hear the last part of that sentence correctly?"

"Which we *are going to make*."

"You once told me that this family was a democracy."

"Wrong. I said that this family is a benevolent dictatorship."

"Don't I get any part in the decision making? Is this a fascist state?"

"Not at all. You get a part."

"What part?"

"You're going to help us choose a house."

*

They sat around the table in the living room, which had once been the dining room table until the dining room had become Sam's bedroom. It was certainly true, Anastasia thought again, that the apartment was getting too small. Or maybe they were getting too big. Certainly *she* was getting too big. Five foot seven, for pete's sake. Probably the Celtics would be scouting her for their basketball team before she was fifteen. At this rate she would be almost seven feet tall by then. Already no boys liked her, because she was taller than they were. When she was seven feet tall, it would be even worse.

Not that she *wanted* any boys to like her. Anastasia hated all boys, especially all the boys in the sixth grade of the Bosler Elementary School, and most especially Robert Giannini, who carried a briefcase to school every day. She wondered what Robert Giannini did with his briefcase now that school was over for the summer.

Maybe there would be more interesting boys in junior high in the fall. Not that she cared, of course.

And by fall, they might be living in the suburbs. She could feel the thought of it affecting her physically. The stomachache was coming back. She could feel her hair beginning to ooze oil, so she would have to wash it again before she went to bed, and she had already washed it that morning. She could feel a pimple beginning to grow on her chin. Her eyes, behind her glasses, began to blur. Terrific. Now she was going blind on top of everything else.

Anastasia pictured herself in the suburbs: seven feet tall, with acne and greasy hair, and blind. She would get a Seeing Eye dog, a ferocious one, and name him Fang. If any boys ever made any remarks to her about her height, she would simply say in a low voice to Fang, "Kill."

That wasn't a bad thought. It made her smile to herself. She pictured her Seeing Eye dog tearing Robert Giannini's briefcase to shreds with his teeth and then starting in on Robert Giannini himself. She grinned. Her vision came back.

"So," said her father, taking out a notebook, "what we need to do is make a list."

Anastasia groaned. Even her mother groaned. Dr. Krupnik was always making lists. Once, when Anastasia was younger, *she* had been a list maker, too. But then her life became too complicated.

"House," wrote Dr. Krupnik at the top of the page. "Okay," he said. "Let's decide what kinds of things we want to look for in a house. Katherine, what's most important to you?"

Her mother thought for a moment, chewing on a strand of her long hair. Her hair was always shiny, like a TV commercial for shampoo. She didn't even wash it every day. She told Anastasia that when she was a teen-ager, she had had oily hair, but Anastasia didn't believe her. Parents always tell you stuff to make you feel better, and when they do, it makes you feel worse.

"Light," said her mother, finally. "Good light, and a room all to myself, where I can paint."

That made sense. Anastasia had been afraid for a moment that her mother would say, "Coppertone appliances in the kitchen." Anybody who had a kitchen full of coppertone appliances would very soon start wearing big pink curlers and worrying about wax build-up.

But light, good light, and a room where she could paint made sense. Anastasia's mother was a very good painter. Long ago, before she was married, she had studied art in New York. Even now some of her paintings hung in galleries in Boston and Cambridge. But her easel and paints were in the tiny room that had once been a pantry. She never complained about that, but it made Anastasia feel a little sad for her.

"Light," wrote Dr. Krupnik on the page. "Room for painting," he wrote. "Anastasia?" he asked. "What is most important to you?"

She was thinking. Now that her vision had unblurred, now that she wasn't going blind, she wouldn't need the Seeing Eye dog. Probably there was a law against having a Seeing Eye dog if you could see. Still, she did like the idea of a monstrous dog, straining at the end of a leash, to whom she could whisper, "Kill," if someone like Robert Giannini started making remarks.

"You go next, Dad," said Anastasia. "I'm still thinking."

"Study," he wrote next. "Bookcases," he wrote beside it.

Well, that made sense, too. Dr. Krupnik was a professor of English. He also wrote poetry, and each time he had written enough poems to make a book, he sent them off to his publisher, and then a new book was published with his name on it. His picture was on the back of each of his books. Anastasia could never figure out why people didn't recognize him on the streets and rush up and ask for his autograph. But they didn't. He said he didn't mind; in fact, he said, he was *glad* that they didn't.

People wrote to him, though. Strangers wrote to him: people who had read his books of poetry. Once, a year ago, Anastasia had gotten into a *lot* of trouble because of those letters. One night at dinner, when Sam was a much younger baby who kept them all awake at night because he howled and screamed a lot, so they were all feeling tired, Dr. Krupnik had said, "There is a stack of mail on my desk that is giving me gray hair."

"Dad," Anastasia had pointed out, "you don't *have* any hair." That was true. The top of his head was quite bald.

"Well, my beard is getting gray, from that mail. When am I ever going to find time to answer it? I have to correct three hundred exams, and the publisher wants revisions on the new book . . ."

"Oh, don't worry," said her mother. "You'll get to it sometime. Those people don't expect answers anyway."

He had just groaned and stroked his beard.

Anastasia had thought about that. She *liked* to write letters, and she never had anyone to write to, because no one ever wrote to her. So the next day, using her father's portable typewriter, she had answered all of the letters. It was fun. To the man in Des Moines, who had sent three poems, asking Dr. Krupnik to read them and give his opinion, Anastasia wrote:

> Dear Mr. Covington,
>   I read all of your nice poems. They are very nice. They are not as good as mine, but that is because I have worked a long time at it, and I am quite famous. Maybe if you work at it some more, yours will be better in the future. I certainly do hope so.

A girl had written a very peculiar letter from San Francisco. The letter said that Myron Krupnik's love poems had really spoken to where she was at, and she thought they had kindred souls, and she would like to spend some time with him if he was ever in San Francisco. Anastasia answered her:

Dear Lisa,
I am a married man with two adorable children. And I never go to San Francisco. But thank you anyway.

A librarian in Detroit had written that Dr. Krupnik's new book was very popular in her library. It was amazing, she wrote, how often people checked it out. Anastasia answered the librarian:

... I don't think it is amazing at all. It is, after all, one of the finest collections of poetry published in the twentieth century. I wish you would suggest to them, though, that they *buy* the book. I don't make any money when they take it out of the library. If they buy it, I make 10%.

There had been twelve letters, and Anastasia had answered all of them, and she had mailed her answers. When she had told her father that night what she had done, she had planned to suggest that he might pay her a secretarial salary. It had taken her all day to write the letters. Even at minimum wage, it would be a good chunk of money for her savings account.

Instead, he had gone storming out of the house to the post office to try to get her letters back. The post office people had let him in, even though they were closed, but they wouldn't give him the letters. They told him that tampering with the mails was a federal offense. So he

came home and drank two beers, very fast, without of-
fering Anastasia the foam — without even *speaking* to
Anastasia, for that matter — and then he stayed up until
2:00 A.M. writing letters to all the same people that
Anastasia had just written to.

Anastasia had not figured out why her father was so
upset until a few weeks later, when it became very clear.
Robert Giannini had slipped her a note in school. The
note said, "I like you. Do you like me? Check one: Yes.
No. A whole lot. I hate you. I don't know." She had
checked "I hate you" immediately; then she had decided
that was cruel. So she erased her first check mark and
checked, simply, "No." Underneath, she had written,
"Sorry."

But she had thought, suddenly, while she was answer-
ing it, about how her father might have answered if he
had tried to do it for her. Her father didn't believe in
what he called "terse negatives." That meant that he
didn't like simple nos. He probably would have written
some long boring response, beginning "Dear Robert, you
are in many ways a fine person, but at this particular
time . . ."

Thinking about it, she had begun to realize that people just can't answer other people's mail.

Her parents were looking at her, and she realized that
she had been daydreaming again, and not even about
the right thing, not about the new house. What a horrible thought, a new house. Even thinking about Robert
Giannini was better than thinking about a new house.

"What would happen," she asked slowly, "if we made

this list about what we want in a house, and then we couldn't find a house that had those things?"

"Well," said her father, "I suppose we'd have to give up and stay here. But I think we can probably find what we want. Look: we've put down a room for your mom to paint in, with lots of light. And a study for me, with bookcases. While your mind was drifting there, off in space somewhere, we added a yard, for Sam. Can't you think of anything that *you* want, Anastasia?"

"Yes," said Anastasia, realizing suddenly that she had solved everything, that they would not have to leave the apartment, not have to live in the suburbs after all. "A tower. I want a house where I can have a room in a tower."

To her surprise, her father wrote that down.

*

"The Mystery of the Girl Who Lived in a Tower," Anastasia wrote dreamily.

Then she looked at that title. Good grief. It sounded like a Nancy Drew title. Probably on the library shelf of twelve thousand Nancy Drew books, there was already one called "The Mystery of the Tower Room" or something.

She tore that page out of her notebook and threw it away. It was much harder to write a book than she had ever realized it would be.

"Telephone for you, Anastasia!" her mother called from the kitchen.

Anastasia put down her book and walked toward the kitchen, thumping her hand along the wall.

"Who is it?" she asked her mother.

"I don't know. I didn't ask."

"Boy or girl?" What a dumb question. *Boys* never called her.

"Girl." Of course.

She took the receiver and stretched the cord so that she could take the phone into the pantry.

"Hello?"

"Hi, Anastasia. This is Robert."

"*Who?*"

"Robert Giannini."

"Oh. I thought it was a girl."

Good grief. What an incredibly dumb thing to say. It wasn't Robert Giannini's fault that his voice still sounded like a girl's. Anastasia sat down on the pantry floor and wanted to die on the spot.

"No, it's Robert." Maybe he hadn't noticed the incredibly dumb thing she had said.

"Hi, Robert."

"Hi."

If only she had paid more attention to the *Cosmopolitan* article on being a spritely conversationalist. It had had a section about Phone Flirtation. Not that she cared.

Robert wasn't very spritely at conversation either, for pete's sake. Now they had each said hi twice, and no one was saying anything.

"I was just wondering the other day," Anastasia said, finally, "what you do with your briefcase in the summertime." Good grief. What an idiotic thing to say. As if she'd been *thinking* about him, or something.

"I keep stuff in it. I collect stuff."

"Oh."

"You want to go collect stuff with me?"

"What do you mean?"

"Well, do you want to go ride bikes and maybe go down by the river and see if there's any interesting junk lying around?"

"Oh. Well, okay."

"Today do you want to do it?"

"Yeah, okay."

"I'll meet you down at your corner. In about an hour, okay? I could come sooner but I have to take a shower first."

"Okay. Good-by."

Anastasia groaned after she hung up the phone. If only he hadn't said that about the shower. The absolutely last thing in the entire world that Anastasia wanted to know was that Robert Giannini was taking a shower, for pete's sake. It was the most embarrassing thing she had ever heard.

She wandered back into her bedroom, looked around at the clothes strewn on the floor, and had a horrible thought. She had nothing to wear. The jeans she was wearing had paint on one knee. Everything on the floor or the bed or the chair — or in the closet, for that matter — was either too small, or incredibly ugly, or else Robert Giannini had already seen her wearing it.

Maybe she should call him back and tell him she couldn't go. But then he would ask why, and she would have to say she had no clothes, and that would be too embarrassing.

She wandered back to the kitchen. Her mother was defrosting the refrigerator. Sam was sitting on the floor, wearing only a diaper and sucking on chunks of ice that had come loose from the freezer.

"I'm eating ice," said Sam matter-of-factly. Sam had a knack for saying things that were already completely obvious, like, "I wet my diapers," or "I'm eating my dinner," or "I'm wearing my pajamas with clowns on them."

"I can *see* that you're eating ice, Sam," Anastasia said

sarcastically. "Mom, you haven't by any chance bought me any new clothes recently and forgotten to tell me, have you?"

Her mother brushed back her hair from her eyes with one hand. "Nope. Why would I do that?"

"I don't know. I just hoped that you had. I don't have anything to wear."

"Are you going someplace?"

"Yeah, I'm just going out to ride bikes with a friend of mine. No big deal."

"What's wrong with what you're wearing?"

"Yuck. Look: paint on my knee. And this shirt has a torn sleeve."

"Well, it's pretty hot out. Why don't you wear your jogging shorts?"

"*Mom.* You can see my *legs* in them."

Her mother looked puzzled. "Of *course* you can see your legs in them. You can see *anybody's* legs in jogging shorts."

"Well, my legs are too skinny, if you must know."

Her mother sighed. "There's a clean pair of jeans in your drawer. If those won't do, I don't have any other suggestions. Unless you want to wear a dress."

Anastasia thumped back down the hall, into her room, and unfolded the clean jeans from her drawer. She put them on. They weren't too bad. She pulled a shirt out of the drawer, started to put it on, suddenly realized what it said, and wadded it back into the drawer. "Boston is for Lovers" was what the shirt said. Good grief. What if

24

she had actually *worn* a shirt that said "Boston is for Lovers" across the front when she went to meet Robert Giannini, the jerk? It made her face feel hot to think about it.

Now she was *quite* sure that a pimple was starting on her chin. Her chin felt huge. She looked in the mirror; nothing on her chin except a couple of ugly freckles. Well, she was sure it was there, lurking, under the freckles. Probably it would *appear* just as she met Robert. She would be standing there and all of a sudden, right when he was looking at her, this *thing* would come bursting out of her chin. Probably he would *say* something about it, that jerk.

Anastasia found a shirt she didn't hate too much, one with a hideous frog on the front, and she pulled it on over her head. Now her hair was a mess. No time to wash her hair. She had washed it last night but already it felt as if she had washed it in Crisco Oil.

Anastasia groaned, called "See you" to her mother and to Sam, and went off to get her bike out of the garage.

*

"Hi."

"Hi."

Terrific. It was going to be just like the telephone conversation.

"Have you been having a good summer, Anastasia?" Robert sounded just like her great-aunt who called sometimes from Milwaukee.

"Okay, I guess. I think we're going to move."

"You're going to *move?* Where are you going to move to?"

"Someplace out in the suburbs, I guess. We're looking for a house."

Robert wrinkled his nose. Anastasia wasn't sure if he was making a face about moving to the suburbs, or if he had to wrinkle his nose to adjust his glasses. Sometimes she did that to adjust her glasses, especially if it was hot.

"That's lousy," Robert said sympathetically. "You'll have to go to a new school and everything, and you won't know anybody. You won't have any friends."

Boy. Some people really know just what to say to cheer you up.

"I don't think I want to talk about it," said Anastasia glumly.

"Well, come on then," said Robert. "Let's ride down to the river." They got on their bikes. Robert had his briefcase hooked onto the back of his. Typical, thought Anastasia, looking at the briefcase. *Typical.*

The Charles River separated Cambridge from Boston. From their side, they could look across and see the sky-scrapers of the city. Anastasia loved Boston, but she loved her side of the river more, where the old brick buildings of Harvard stood. Her father taught at Harvard. He rode a bike to work each day, and he carried a briefcase with him on his bike, but that was okay because he was forty-seven.

Her mother's bike had a little seat for Sam, and that was okay, too. In fact, her parents were perfect Cambridge people, Anastasia thought. Lots of Cambridge men had beards, as her father did, and rode bikes to work. Lots of Cambridge mothers wore jeans and rode bikes with baby seats to the grocery store, as her mother did. Nobody stared, in Cambridge, at her mother's clothes, like the French tee shirt with the picture of the chicken, and under the chicken an oval with the word *oeuf* in it. *Oeuf* meant "egg" in French. Anastasia's mother spoke French. She had spent a year in Paris, painting, before she was married.

Not one single person in the suburbs would know what *oeuf* meant. Anastasia was absolutely certain of that.

The banks of the Charles were filled with people. There were always lots of people there on warm days, all sorts of people. College students lying on blankets, reading. Families with babies and small children. Black people, white people, Chinese people, people who spoke other languages. Anastasia liked looking at the Indians best; the women wore long, flowing dresses that were not really dresses at all, but pieces of bright cloth wrapped around them in a complicated way. Some of them had a single red spot decorating the center of their forehead. Their husbands wore turbans and had bushy beards and mustaches that came to points at the sides. Two of the turbaned men were throwing a Frisbee back and forth, and between them a dark-skinned baby toddled, wearing Pampers.

Anastasia wondered if there were drugstores in India, with shelves of Pampers and Vitalis and Crest toothpaste.

She and Robert leaned their bikes against a tree. Near them, two girls speaking French were trying to put a kite together. They were doing it wrong, and Anastasia could have told them how to do it right, but the only French she knew was *oeuf* and *merci*.

Robert had unhooked his briefcase, and she saw him pick something up from under a bush and stash it away quickly in the briefcase.

"What was that?" she asked.

"Nothing. Just junk."

Liar. She had seen that it was a *Playboy* magazine.

"What kind of stuff do you usually find?"

"Last week I found a piece of rope and a plastic wine glass. Once I found a dollar bill."

A dollar bill. That wouldn't be so bad. She walked along beside Robert. There were a lot of things on the grass, but none of them very interesting. Squashed beer cans. Paper napkins. Flattened cigarette packs. A little plastic car with the wheels missing: she picked that up. Sam would like it. She put it in her pocket.

"Robert, you want a sock?"

Robert looked startled, as if she were going to hit him. "What for?"

"No, I don't mean I'm going to sock you. Do you want a *sock*, the kind you wear? There's one lying over there."

"What color?" He didn't see it.

"Gray. But that's from dirt. I think it's probably white."

"I guess not. One sock's not very useful."

"You could hang it up at Christmas." Good grief. She wished she hadn't said that. She didn't want Robert to know that she still hung up a stocking at Christmas, like a baby.

But Robert grinned. "I use my mom's pantyhose at Christmas. She wears the stretchable kind."

Anastasia giggled. She happened to know that Robert's mother was quite fat. She wondered if Mrs. Giannini wore the kind of pantyhose that Anastasia had seen at the supermarket, the ones called Fat Fanny pantyhose.

Of course she couldn't ask Robert that.

It was weird, the difference between talking to boys and talking to girls. Anastasia couldn't figure that out. She could have mentioned Fat Fanny pantyhose to her best friend, Jenny MacCauley. But in a million years she wouldn't have mentioned Fat Fanny pantyhose to Robert.

But her mother didn't seem to have that problem, talking to her father. Or talking to any of their men friends, in fact. Her mother could have said Fat Fanny pantyhose as if it were just an ordinary, funny thing to say.

What made it different, talking to Robert? Anastasia decided to read the *Cosmopolitan* article when she got home, the one about making spritely conversation, to see whether it explained why there are certain people that you have trouble saying stuff to, and why it feels, when you are with those people, as if your tongue is too big.

"You want to sit down and watch the boats?" asked Robert. They had walked quite a distance along the river. Robert had collected a few things: the *Playboy* that he thought she hadn't seen; a paperback copy of Shakespeare's sonnets, which he said he would give to his grandmother; a broken belt buckle, which he thought he could fix; and a whole batch of Popsicle sticks, which he said he used for building things like model airplanes. Anastasia only had the little plastic car in her pocket and a matchbook from the Hyatt Regency.

They sat down, and Robert began to fool with one of his sneakers. Anastasia began to pray. She did not pray very often — only when absolutely necessary — but it was absolutely necessary right now. She prayed that Robert was not going to take his sneakers off. Anastasia thought that feet were the grossest things in the whole world. If she had to look at Robert Giannini's feet, she would die, right there on the banks of the Charles River.

But he was only dislodging a pebble. Thank you, God, said Anastasia to herself.

"How is your family?" asked Robert politely.

"They're okay. My father's teaching a couple of summer school courses. And my mother just finished doing some illustrations for a book about seashells."

"Don't you have a baby brother? I remember when we were in fourth grade, your mom had a baby."

"Yeah. Sam. He's . . ." Anastasia hesitated. It was hard to describe Sam. "He's kind of weird," she said, finally.

Robert looked puzzled.

"He can talk okay," Anastasia said.

"Why is he weird, then?"

Good grief. It would be easy to explain, if she could tell about how Sam wasn't toilet trained. But she couldn't say *that*, to Robert, any more than she could say Fat Fanny pantyhose. Then she remembered what her father had said about Sam.

"Some parts of him didn't develop as quickly as others," she told Robert. "His brain is in good shape. But some other parts of him aren't so good."

"Oh," said Robert. "I understand."

They sat silently and watched the boats. The river was dotted with small sailboats, heeled over in the breeze. Anastasia thought that it would be fun to be in a sailboat. She didn't know how to sail. But she thought that it would be fun just to be a passenger, just to be sitting in the boat, maybe trailing her fingers in the water, while Robert did the sailing . . .

Good grief. Anastasia almost blushed. She had actually been thinking about sailing with dumb Robert Giannini, the jerk. Probably he would bring his briefcase along on a sailboat, for pete's sake.

"You know," said Robert, "I've never told anybody this . . ."

Oh no, thought Anastasia. I don't want him to tell me something that he's never told anybody, for pete's sake.

". . . but I have this cousin."

"So?"

"Well, my cousin Pete, he's sixteen years old. He's my aunt Marie's son?"

"Yeah."

"And he's retarded."

"That's too bad," said Anastasia politely.

Robert was poking the grass with a twig. "I mean, he's

really very severely retarded. He can't even live at home. He lives at a special place. Sometimes Aunt Maries takes him out for the day. Sometimes she brings him to our house. And he's just like practically a baby or something. He can't even feed himself."

"That's too bad," said Anastasia politely again. She felt genuinely sad about Robert's cousin Pete.

"So, well, the reason I told you that, is because you shouldn't feel too bad about Sam. Because you said his brain is okay, and that's really the important thing. It doesn't matter that he's deformed. You shouldn't feel embarrassed about that or anything."

Deformed? Good grief. Had she said that Sam was deformed? Why had she said *that?* And now that she had said it, and Robert had made that long speech about his cousin, and he had never told anybody else, for pete's sake, now she certainly couldn't say hey, I made a mistake, I lied, Sam *isn't* deformed.

"Yeah, well, I'm not embarrassed about it," she said miserably. "It's not that bad."

"And you know they can do a lot of good stuff at Children's Hospital. Probably your parents have already taken him there."

"Yeah, they have." That, at least, wasn't a lie. Sam had had X rays at Children's Hospital last year, when he tipped over his high chair and fell on his head. The X rays were negative. He was fine. It took a long time to wash the oatmeal out of his hair, though.

❖

Robert said good-by to Anastasia at the corner near her house. He said he was going to go home and make something out of his Popsicle sticks. He also said two other things that made her feel strange.

One was, "If you move to someplace not too far away, I'll ride out on my bike to see you."

She answered, "Okay."

And the other was, "My family always donates money to the March of Dimes and stuff."

She couldn't figure out why he said that. "That's nice," she said, puzzled. "Mine gives money to the Civil Liberties Union."

"The March of Dimes goes to help crippled children, like Sam," Robert explained before he rode away.

Anastasia walked her bike down the block to where she lived. She decided that she would definitely read that article in *Cosmopolitan*. Maybe it would explain how some people got themselves into such dumb situations by simply opening their mouths. Maybe it would explain how to get *out* of those situations.

She wondered how she would go about hiding Sam if Robert did come to visit her in the suburbs.

＊

It was all too complicated, too mysterious. She couldn't begin to make a title out of all the things that were mystifying in her life.

Maybe she should write a letter to "Dear Abby," instead.

"Dear Abby," Anastasia wrote, "There is this boy in my

class, I'll call him Richard to protect his identity, and the first thing that went wrong today was that Richard called me, and I said incredibly dumb things on the phone, and then . . ."

She stopped. Dear Abby would laugh. Anastasia had a sudden, horrible vision of Dear Abby, looking glamorous, sitting behind a mahogany desk, reading Anastasia's letter and wiping tears off her cheeks with a lace handkerchief, because she was laughing so hard that she cried. Then she would publish the letter in the newspaper, and everyone in Anastasia's school — everyone in Cambridge, in fact — would read it and would recognize who it was, because of course she would have to write about the briefcase. Everyone in Cambridge would laugh at her.

She turned to a new page in her notebook. "The Mystery," she wrote, thinking in titles again, "of Why Other People Always Think Your Very Serious Problems Are Hysterically Funny."

"Run a comb through your hair, sport. The real estate lady'll be here in half an hour. She's going to take us to look at a house."

"Daddy, I *told* you I don't want to go and look at houses. *Casablanca* is on TV this afternoon. I'm going to watch it over at Jenny's. You and Mom go look at the house with the real estate lady. I'll take Sam with me to Jenny's if you want."

"Nope. You and Sam are coming with us today. Your mom and I have already looked at seven houses . . ."

Her mother interrupted. "I looked at five others without you, Myron. I've looked at twelve altogether."

"Twelve, then. And this sounds like one that we want

35

you to see. And Sam, too. Where is Sam?"

Anastasia groaned and went to look for her brother. She found him sitting on his bedroom floor looking at a volume of *War and Peace*.

"Good grief, Sam. Don't tell me you can *read* now!"

"Of course I can't read. I'm only two and a half years old. I'm looking for the pictures. Why doesn't this book have pictures?"

"I don't know. Probably pictures hadn't been invented yet, when it was written. Come on, Sam. Let me change your diaper. We have to go look at a house."

"Booorrrring," said Sam cheerfully.

"You're right: *boring*. Hey, listen Sam. Do you want to have a plot?"

"Okay."

"Well, you cry when you see the house, okay? Cry a whole lot, and say you hate it. Say you're *allergic* to it. Say it makes your eyes hurt, or something."

"Okay," said Sam cheerfully. He practiced a fake whimper.

"Yeah, that's pretty good," said Anastasia as she changed his diaper and buttoned him into a clean sunsuit. "Just keep doing that when you see the house. Maybe you can make real tears."

❁

The real estate lady had bleached hair and a gross car with push-button windows. Sam fooled with the button on his window and mashed his fingers and began to cry.

"Not yet, Sam," muttered Anastasia. "Save it."

"I think you'll adore this house," said the real estate lady in a fake voice. "Good neighborhood, too. Wonderful schools. What grade did you say you were in, Anastasia?"

"I'll be in seventh."

"Oh, goodness, I thought you were older. Maybe because you're so tall for your age."

Terrific. Didn't anybody ever tell her how rude it is to mention somebody's *flaws,* for pete's sake? Was she going to mention her father's baldness next?

No. She was going to talk about the roof and the furnace. Wonderful old slate roof, needs no maintenance at all, lasts forever; wonderful brand new furnace, just put in last year, hardly uses any oil, blah blah blah. Anastasia could hardly believe that her mother had been through this twelve times already. She tried to think of the most boring thing she had ever done; going to an organ concert at the Catholic church with Jenny MacCauley's family came to her mind. She had almost fallen asleep. She imagined doing it twelve times. No way.

And this was just as boring, maybe even more so. Now the lady was babbling about the plumbing, the wonderful copper pipes, the woodwork, the wonderful woodwork, the interest rates, the wonderful interest rates.

Anastasia's interest rate in this conversation was zero percent. She leaned back on the gross plastic seat of the gross car and gazed through the window.

The trees and lawns were nice. It was sure a lot greener than Cambridge.

"Look, Sam," she said, and pointed. Some kids in bathing suits were running through a sprinkler in a yard.

Sam looked. "I would like that," he said thoughtfully.

"Yeah, because you like being wet, dummy," Anastasia said pointedly.

Anastasia was beginning to feel very odd. At first she thought maybe she was carsick. Then she realized what it was. It was because she liked what she was seeing through the windows of the car. She liked the trees and the lawns and the flowers. She liked the idea of running through a sprinkler, even with dumb Sam. She liked it that there were dogs and kids and bikes and a kind of nice-smelling quiet out here, wherever they were. But to like those things meant moving, and she loved Cambridge and the apartment. So there was a war going on in her stomach.

"Well, kiddos," said the real estate lady in her Barbie Doll voice, as she turned a corner, "here we are. This is it!"

Sam dutifully burst into fake tears. "I'm allergic to it!" he wailed.

Anastasia didn't even hear him. She was looking at the house, and her stomach felt as if she had been kicked by someone wearing cowboy boots. Her mother had once told her that it was painful to fall in love, and now, suddenly, she knew what that meant. She had expected to feel it for the first time when she fell in love with a *boy*, for pete's sake. But now she was feeling it — the pain in her stomach, her heart beating funny, Mantovani violin music in her ears, and aching behind her eyes as she tried not to cry — because she was falling in love with a *house*.

It was because the house had a tower.

*

And it happened to all of them as if it were a contagious disease. The main symptoms were speechlessness and silly grins.

The real estate lady didn't understand that. She thought something was wrong. She became confused when none of them said anything, and she began to apologize for the house.

The study was lined from floor to ceiling, on every wall, with bookcases. And it had a fireplace. Anastasia's father stood in the center of the study with a silly grin and said nothing.

"I know you wanted a study," said the real estate lady. "Of course this room seems small, I know. But you could have all these shelves torn out, and that would open up the room quite a bit and make it larger, and . . ."

Her voice drifted away in confusion, because no one was listening to her. Anastasia could read her father's mind. In his mind he was arranging all his books, alphabetically, in the shelves. In his mind, he had a roaring fire in the fireplace; he was sitting in front of it, smoking his pipe, reading.

They moved on to another room, a huge octagonal room stuck onto the side of the house. It was all windows. They stood there, silently, with the same silly grins, and Anastasia read her mother's mind. Her mother was setting up easels in the room. She was doing huge paintings with sweeping brush strokes. She was hiring models to stand there in the brilliant light. She was doing sculpture. Murals.

The real estate lady began to talk very fast, trying to mend the silence. "Of course, in the Victorian era, when this house was built, they always had these strange rooms that they called solariums. Useless, now. You could close it off to conserve heat. Or, in fact, you could even have this room torn down. It does stick out rather awkwardly, from the side of the house, I know. The yard would be bigger if you just had this room taken off, and . . ."

But no one was listening to her. She stopped talking, mid-sentence, confused, and they moved on.

Upstairs, they moved from one bedroom to another. Big bedrooms, with fireplaces and huge closets for playing hide-and-seek. Their feet echoed in the empty rooms: the heavy, decisive steps of Dr. Krupnik's size-twelve shoes; the staccato taps of the real estate lady's high heels; the duet of Anastasia's sneakers and her mother's sandals; and behind them, the pad, pad, pad of Sam's little feet.

Now not even the real estate lady was saying much. She was embarrassed. She thought they hated the house. Halfheartedly, in a bathroom, she said, "New plumbing. Wonderful copper pipes," but then she fell silent again and looked through her pocketbook for a cigarette.

Finally, she opened a door on the second floor and gestured toward the narrow, curving staircase behind it.

"You could just close this off," she said, and puffed nervously on her cigarette.

Anastasia scuttled up the little staircase alone to the tower room and stood there looking out and down, at the green lawns, the huge elms, the curving streets, and in the distance, the Charles River and the buildings of Cambridge and Boston.

Her parents didn't come up the stairs. They had read her mind and knew that she wanted to be in the tower room alone.

But after a moment she could hear Sam's small feet climbing the stairs. He appeared in the room, looking puzzled, and said, "Do you want me to cry again? Do you want to do the plot now?"

But Anastasia said no and took his hand. They went back downstairs just in time to hear her father tell the real estate lady that they would buy the house.

*

"The Mystery," wrote Anastasia carefully, "of Why You Sometimes Hate the Idea of Something, but Then You Like the Thing Itself."

Now that had possibilities for a book. She would have to refine the title a little, because it seemed a little complicated. But it had real possibilities.

Below the title, after she reflected on the possibilities, she wrote, "Subtitle: Or Why You Sometimes *Like* the Idea of Something, But Hate the Thing Itself."

Moving, and the new house, seemed to fall into the first category. And Robert Giannini seemed to fall into the second.

41

5

"Boy, Anastasia, I don't know," said Jenny. "I said I'd
help you pack. And I *will* help you pack." She put a stack
of Anastasia's paperback books into a carton, halfheartedly. "But boy, Anastasia. I really hate it that you're moving. You've been my best friend ever since we started
kindergarten."

"Yeah," said Anastasia glumly. "Except for that one
summer, when Lindsay Cavanaugh moved in down the
street."

"Yeah, Lindsay Cavanaugh, that jerk."

"She was your best friend that whole summer. I
wanted to kill myself."

"Yeah. You know why it was, though. Her father was a

filmmaker, remember? He was going to use Lindsay and me in a movie."

"Big deal."

"Yeah, big deal. We had to get up at 5:00 A.M., and he took us out to Crane's Beach, and we had to run on the beach with no clothes on while he took movies. When my father found out he did that, he almost broke old Lindsay Cavanaugh's father's neck."

"Yeah, I remember." Anastasia giggled. "It wasn't porno or anything, though. You were only seven years old, for pete's sake."

"Actually, it was probably a pretty good movie. The sun was coming up and everything, and we were the only people on the beach. Except birds. Nobody ever got to see it, though, because my father made him destroy the film."

"I sure hated you that summer. You were so conceited."

"Well, I thought I was a big movie star. Except for that summer, we've always been best friends. Are you taking this, or throwing it away?" She held up a battered arithmetic book.

"Good grief. Where did you find that?"

"It was under your bed."

"I thought I lost it. My mother had to pay the school for it. I guess you'd better throw it out."

The arithmetic book sailed into the big trash can that was in the middle of Anastasia's room.

"Can I have this picture of you? I don't want to forget what you look like." Jenny had a Polaroid snapshot of Anastasia in her hand.

"Sure, but it's ugly. And you're not going to forget what I look like anyway, Jenny. Aren't you going to come visit me? Robert Giannini said that he was going . . ." Anastasia stopped talking abruptly, and blushed.

"Who? *Robert Giannini?* What's Robert Giannini going to do?"

"Nothing."

"What do you mean, nothing? Robert Giannini's going to *visit* you, isn't he, Anastasia? He's going to *visit* you! I can't believe it, that jerk!"

"Do you think I should keep this orangutan poster, or throw it away? I've had it about five years. I'm kind of bored with it."

"Throw it away. And quit changing the subject. Are you going to let that jerk Giannini visit you? Did you *invite* him?"

"No, I didn't invite him. He invited himself. But he isn't so bad, Jenny. He really isn't. He's *kind* of a jerk, but not full-fledged."

Jenny threw herself onto Anastasia's bed, held her stomach, and groaned. "You *like* him, don't you? You actually *like* Robert Giannini! I can't believe it."

"I don't like him. I just don't *hate* him anymore."

"Traitor. Traitor traitor traitor. Why didn't you tell me?"

"I forgot."

"You didn't forget. You were embarrassed."

"Yeah, I was embarrassed."

Jenny lay on the bed with her eyes closed. "Well, guess what."

"What?"

There was a long silence. Then Jenny took a deep breath. "I don't hate Michael Gottlieb anymore, either."

"*That jerk?*"

"He's not really a jerk. Really, he isn't, Anastasia. The other day he came over, and we went down to the store and got Popsicles. He was sort of nice, all of a sudden."

"Why didn't you tell me?"

"I forgot."

"Liar."

Jenny looked at Anastasia and grinned. Anastasia began to laugh. Jenny began to laugh. Anastasia could hardly talk because she was laughing so hard; but finally she sputtered, "Michael Gottlieb! He always wears that stupid baseball cap!" Jenny doubled up, laughing, and gasped, "Robert Giannini! That briefcase! That gross briefcase!"

For the rest of the day, they couldn't look at each other without making the kind of semisneezing noise that holds back a brand new laugh.

*

It was hard, packing. Not hard on the muscles — Anastasia had pretty good muscles — but hard on the head. And hard on the heart.

Anastasia found her mother crying, one afternoon. Not curled-up-on-a-bed, pounding-your-fists-into-the-pillow sort of crying. Just silent, tears-running-down-your-cheeks crying. Her mother was standing in the pantry, packing dishes, and there were tears on her face.

"Did you hurt yourself?"

Her mother sniffed and smiled. "No. I'm just sad."

Anastasia picked up a plate and looked at it. It was an ordinary yellow plate. It made her think of spaghetti and of meat loaf. It didn't make her feel sad.

"If I were you, I would feel good about this plate," she told her mother. "*Most* people in the suburbs eat off of plastic dishes."

"Assumptions again."

"No, really. They do. Except when they eat TV dinners. Those they eat right out of the tin tray."

Her mother leaned against the cupboard and began to laugh. "Anastasia, haven't you figured out yet that your assumptions all turn out to be *wrong?* Take the new house, for example. You thought we'd have to move to a split-level house in a development. Instead we found that wonderful house with a tower."

Anastasia shrugged and grinned.

"How did you become such an expert on suburban life, anyway?"

"Told you. Books and TV. Mostly TV commercials. You never see *city* people worrying about ring-around-the-collar."

"Well, we won't worry about it either, not even when we live in the suburbs."

"Why were the dishes making you cry?"

"It wasn't the dishes. I was feeling sad about the stained glass in these cupboard doors. I've always loved this stained glass."

Anastasia looked at the stained-glass windows of the cupboards. She remembered when Sam was a tiny baby, and they had kept his little crib in the pantry. She used to open the cupboard door, stand behind it, and make faces at the baby. The very first time Sam had smiled was when Anastasia had been making a purple-and-amber face at him, wiggling her nose.

Oh, dear. Now Anastasia was starting to feel sad, too.

She wiggled the loose pane of colored glass. "Maybe we could take it out and take it with us, Mom."

"No. It doesn't belong to us."

"Of *course* it belongs to us! It's always been ours! All my *life* I remember this stained glass!"

"But we don't own this building, or the things that are part of it. So when we leave, we have to leave all these things for the next people who will live here."

Good grief. Anastasia hadn't even thought about someone else living in their apartment. All of a sudden, she thought of the wallpaper in her bedroom. She had chosen it herself, when she was eight. It was blue and white, with people riding old-fashioned bicycles on it; some of them were playing flutes and violins while they rode.

She didn't want anyone else to have that wallpaper. But there was nothing she could do.

Well, there was something. She thumped her way down the echoey hall to her room, which seemed hollow and empty now. The rug was rolled up, and the curtains had been taken down. Her desk, usually cluttered with paint boxes and notebooks and comics, was bare, except for the goldfish bowl where Frank swam lazily back and forth, back and forth.

"Frank," she said, "don't tell anyone that I'm doing this." Frank made a kissing face at her.

Anastasia found a pencil stub in the trash can. She knelt on the bare floor in a corner of the room and wrote, on the wallpaper, in her best printing: "This is my room forever. Anastasia Krupnik."

That made her feel better.

Then she thumped down the hall to her father's study. He was standing beside his own bare desk by the wall with his back to her, and he jumped, startled, when she came in.

He looked guilty. Anastasia was an expert on guilty looks.

"What are you doing, Dad?" she asked.

"Nothing," he said very quickly.

"Nothing" was what you always said when you were doing something that you felt guilty about and someone came along and asked what you were doing. Anastasia was an expert on that. Either you said "nothing," or you whistled, or hummed.

Her father began to hum. He did a little drumming rhythm on his desk top with his fingers.

"You all packed in here?" she asked, looking around the bare room.

"Yep. All ready for the movers. It sure looks empty with the books packed, doesn't it?"

"Yeah. I suppose someone else will move new books in.

Probably their books won't be as good as yours, though."

"Probably no one else will have a first edition of *The Old Man and the Sea*," her father said, and that seemed to make him feel better. "I think I'll have a beer."

He headed for the kitchen. When he was gone, Anastasia saw, suddenly, the place on the wall of the study where, in his best writing, very small, with his fountain pen, he had written his name.

*

Anastasia found Sam in his bedroom, sitting on the floor, crying silently.

"What's wrong, Old Sam?" she asked.

"I'm feeling sad about my blanky," he said.

"Oh, Sam, I'm sorry. I was just teasing when I said your blanky couldn't come to the new house. Of course it can come."

Tears trickled down Sam's cheeks. "But it wants to live here," he whispered to her. "It told me so."

Anastasia thought and thought. "I have an idea, Sam," she said, finally. She ran to the kitchen and got a pair of scissors. Then, sitting beside Sam on his bedroom floor, she carefully cut his ragged yellow blanket in half.

"There," she said. "Now part of it can live here, and part of it can come to the new house." She folded one half and Sam showed her where to put it: on a dark, narrow shelf in the closet. He wrapped the remaining half around his hand, held it against his cheek, and sucked his thumb, testing how it worked with only half. After a moment he smiled. "Okay," he said. "It's okay."

"Good."

"I'm not a baby," he reminded her firmly.

"I know, Sam. I know you're not a baby."

＊

She called Jenny MacCauley on the phone.

"The moving van's coming in about an hour," she said. "So I called to say good-by."

"Will you have a telephone in the new house?"

"Sure."

"Is it long distance?"

"I don't know. Not long distance like Milwaukee, or anything."

"Well, call me and tell me the number."

"I will."

"And call and tell me everything that happens."

"Yeah."

"Like if you meet any boys."

"Okay."

"Or if *Casablanca* ever comes to a movie theater out there, call me, and I'll figure out a way to get there. Don't ever go to *Casablanca* without me, promise."

"I promise. Don't you, either."

"I won't. And if Old Briefcase ever comes to visit, call and tell me."

Anastasia giggled. "Okay."

"Or if you get any new clothes, or anything."

"Okay. And you, Jenny, if you read any good books, call and tell me. Or if Michael Gottlieb comes over. Old Baseball Cap."

Jenny giggled.

"I still can't believe you're moving, Anastasia."

"Me neither. Come and visit me."

"I will."

"Promise."

"I promise."

Then, suddenly, Anastasia was too sad to talk any more. Very quickly, before she began to cry, she said good-by and hung up the telephone.

❖

Everything was packed, and the moving van was pulling up to the front door.

But Anastasia hadn't packed Frank Goldfish — she was going to carry him with her, in his bowl, to the new house — and she hadn't packed her notebook.

Now she sat down on the bare floor, beside Frank in his bowl, and looked around. The moving men were coming in, and she could hear their heavy footsteps on the bare floor of the apartment. Her entire life was packed into cardboard boxes, except for the life that she was leaving here.

"The Mystery," she wrote quickly, before they got to her room, "of Saying Good-by."

She reread it with satisfaction. Now *that*, she thought happily, is a *title*.

6

Anastasia's mother was sitting in the kitchen of the new house in a rocking chair, with her sandals kicked off and her long hair frizzy from the heat.

"Look at me," she said dramatically to Anastasia, who had wandered into the kitchen for a peanut butter sandwich, "and you are looking at someone who is suffering."

"Suffering from what?" asked Anastasia, as she spread peanut butter on a slice of whole wheat bread.

"Angst. And sore feet. And heat stroke."

"And the heartbreak of psoriasis?"

"No. The heartbreak of not being able to find anything. Have you seen a pitcher? Can you tell me how to make iced tea, which I desperately want, without a pitcher?"

"No." Anastasia licked the edges of her sandwich to even them off.

"*Damn.*" Her mother stood up and began to look through a half-unpacked carton.

Her father came into the kitchen, wiping his face with a handkerchief. "Did you make the iced tea?" he asked.

"I don't want to talk about it," said her mother tensely.

"I'm not asking you to talk about it. I'm asking you to pour it."

Her mother glowered at him.

"She can't find a pitcher," Anastasia explained. "Here," she said to her mother, handing her a saucepan. "Use this."

Her father sat down in the rocker, leaned his elbows on his knees, and looked at the floor.

"What's wrong, Dad?" Anastasia happened to know that her father was not at all interested in floors. Whenever he stared at the floor, it meant that something was wrong.

"I was unpacking the records," he said, "and I can't find the Verdi Requiem. I think the movers stole it."

"Dad," said Anastasia patiently. "Those movers never even *heard* of the Verdi Requiem. Those movers were the sort of people who would only steal Peter Frampton."

Her father wasn't paying any attention to her. He was only paying attention to the floor. "Also," he said, "I hate the car. And the car hates me. It backfires at me. It keeps running after I turn the ignition off, even after I get out, and as soon as I am *behind* it, it backfires at me."

"I don't hate the car," said Anastasia cheerfully. "I thought I would, but I don't. I'm glad you got an old beat-up car instead of a gross Cadillac or something."

"Here," said her mother, and handed them each a glass of iced tea. "If it tastes like aluminum, it's not my fault. I think the movers stole all my pitchers."

She sat down in a chair across from Anastasia's father, took a sip of tea, and made a face. Then she put her elbows on her knees and stared at the floor.

"You people are both suffering from Post-moving Depression," announced Anastasia.

"For pete's sake, where did you come up with *that* idea?" asked her mother.

"*Cosmopolitan* magazine."

Her father set his glass on the table with a thud that almost broke it. "Anastasia Krupnik," he said, "we have subscriptions to at least seven magazines in this household, all of them with some intellectual content. Why do you insist upon spending your allowance to buy that garbage?"

"It tells me stuff."

"*What* stuff?"

"Well, one issue had an article about lopsided breasts, how to disguise them, and also an article about wives who get fed up with things and run away. Those might be useful bits of information to me someday."

Her father made a noise like a horse exhaling. He stood up and stomped out of the kitchen.

"Post-moving Depression," said Anastasia to her mother. "It will only last a few days."

54

Sam padded into the kitchen. "I stood in every closet," he said.

"Sam," said his mother. "Where are your sneakers? You're going to get splinters if you don't keep your shoes on." She slid her own feet back into her sandals.

Sam thought. "One sneaker is in one closet," he said, "and one is in a different closet. I forget where." He sat on the floor and examined the soles of his feet. "I *like* splinters," he said happily.

"Sam's not depressed," pointed out Anastasia. "Neither am I. I wonder why the neighbors haven't come to visit, though. Neighbors are supposed to drop in and bring a chocolate cake or something, when you move to a new place."

"I wish someone would drop in and bring a pitcher," muttered her mother. "This tea tastes terrible."

Sam looked up suddenly. "A witch lives next door," he announced.

"No kidding," said Anastasia. "How do you know?"

"I looked out a window, and she was looking out a window."

"How do you know she's a witch? Was she wearing a pointed hat?"

"No," he said, picking some dirt out from between his toes. "She had an ugly witch face."

"Hey," said Anastasia, "I have an idea. We need a pitcher until we find ours, right? Why don't I go next door and borrow a pitcher? That gives me an excuse to meet one neighbor, at least. I'm dying to meet the neighbors."

55

"You want to meet a *witch?*" asked Sam, his eyes lighting up.

"Sure. You want to come, Sam? Find your sneakers and I'll take you with me. I want to comb my hair first."

She was heading out of the kitchen when her mother called her back. "Did it really have that article, the one you said? About wives who just chuck it all and run away? What happens to them? Do they end up happy, living in Malibu or something?"

"Mom," said Anastasia, "just hang in there a couple more days. Post-moving Depression goes away. It really does."

✽

The house next door looked like a Charles Addams house. That didn't bother Anastasia. She even watched the shower scene in *Psycho* without covering her face with her hands, something her mother had never been able to do. She read vampire books and watched late movies about gooey blobs that grew and ate entire city populations, without ever having bad dreams.

But Sam was scared. He wasn't old enough to have developed an immunity to it yet. He held tightly to Anastasia with one hand and tightly to his yellow blanket with another. When they got to the front steps, Sam let go of Anastasia and dropped back to hide behind a bush.

"Dope," she needled him, and left him there. She went up on the porch and pushed hard on the unpolished brass bell. The shrill ring sounded inside the house. After a moment she heard footsteps, slow ones, shuffling.

The door finally opened, and a woman peered out from the dim hall.

Good grief. She really *did* have an ugly witch face. Sam was right. She would have looked perfect on a broom.

"Hello," said Anastasia politely. "I'm your new neighbor. My name is Anastasia Krupnik."

The woman with the witch face stared at her without smiling and didn't say anything. Her gray hair stood out around her face, tangled, like a nest that Anastasia had once seen high in a tree in winter.

"What's your name?" Anastasia asked.

The woman stared at her for another long moment. Finally she said, "Mrs. Stein."

"My mother was wondering if maybe you have a pitcher we could borrow, just for this afternoon until we find ours. We're still unpacking, and it's so hot we need something to make iced tea in."

"No," said Mrs. Stein abruptly. "I don't have one."

Liar. Everybody has a pitcher unless they can't find it.

"Oh," said Anastasia. She wanted to say sarcastically, "Well, thanks anyway, you old bat." But she didn't say that. Instead, she said nicely, "Thank you anyway. I'm sorry I bothered you."

Mrs. Stein began to push the door closed. Then she stopped, looked beyond Anastasia, and said, "Who's *that?*"

Anastasia looked. It was Sam, who had come out from

behind his bush and was looking at them fearfully, his yellow blanket wrapped around his arm and his thumb in his mouth.

"That's my brother, Sam."

"What is that disgusting thing he's holding?"

"It's his blanky. He holds it when he's sleepy or scared."

"Come here, young man," called Mrs. Stein.

Sam climbed the steps to the porch, carefully holding the railing. It took him a long time because he still went up stairs the baby way, with both feet on each step at the same time.

"Do you like cookies?" Mrs. Stein asked him.

Sam nodded.

"How can you eat cookies if you keep your thumb in your mouth?"

Sam removed his thumb and wiped it dry on his blanket.

"Can you talk?"

"Yes," said Sam solemnly.

"My name is Gertrude Stein. Can you say that?"

"Gertrustein," said Sam. He said it the way he said Frankenstein when he was playing monsters.

"Do you prefer chocolate chip cookies or molasses?"

"Both," said Sam.

Gertrude Stein began to laugh. "Come in then, and I'll give you one of each."

She looked sternly at Anastasia. "What was it you said you wanted to borrow?"

"A pitcher."

"You come in, too. I'll give you one." Then, as if she needed to explain something, she said, "I like little children. I do not much care for middle-sized ones."

Anastasia and Sam followed her into the dark house. "This house smells funny," whispered Sam.

It surprised Anastasia that he whispered it. Why was it that Sam, who was only two and a half, already understood something about manners? Some people Sam's age, or even older, would have said that very loudly, which would have been rude. But Sam whispered it, what he said about Gertrustein's house. Anastasia squeezed his hand.

And yet Gertrustein herself, who was probably eighty years older than Sam, had been rude when she opened the door. Or at least she had *seemed* rude.

Anastasia remembered that her grandmother — who had been ninety-two when she died — had sometimes seemed rude.

Maybe it was just that people who were very old, or very young, were the only ones who said exactly what they thought. If they were young, they hadn't learned yet to worry about what other people might think. And if they were old, they didn't care any more.

And the house did smell funny. Sam was right. It wasn't a bad smell; it was just the smell of being closed up: a no-fresh-air-for-a-long-time sort of smell.

"I walk very slowly," said Gertrustein. Anastasia had already noticed that.

"I do, too," said Sam. "It's because I have small legs."

Gertrustein looked back at him and smiled.

Anastasia was surprised again at Sam. He had said something which made her feel good. What a nice guy Sam was beginning to be.

"I don't have small legs," said Gertrustein. "I have big legs, as a matter of fact. But they don't work very well. The doctor says I should go for long walks."

"Do you?" asked Anastasia. "Do you go for long walks?"

"No," sniffed Gertrustein.

The kitchen was not as dim as the rest of the house, because there was sunlight coming in through the windows. But it was very old-fashioned. Gertrustein shuffled over to a thick crockery pot with a lid, opened it, and took out some cookies. She put them on a plate and put the plate on the table.

"There," she said. "Sit down, Sam. You too, girl."

Sam climbed onto a chair and sat with his legs sticking out straight in front of him. Anastasia sat down next to him, and Gertrustein eased herself slowly into a chair and passed the plate of cookies.

"Why don't you go for long walks?" asked Sam, with cookie in his mouth.

"Because," said Gertrustein, with cookie in *her* mouth, "I don't have anyone to walk with, and it is boring to walk all alone."

"Couldn't you go for walks with your friends?" asked Anastasia.

Gertrustein glared at her. "All my friends are dead," she said.

Good grief. There wasn't any cheery answer to *that*, not that Anastasia could think of. Except "I'm sorry," which she said softly.

But Sam looked up, grinning, and said, "*I* could be your friend."

Gertrustein grinned back at him. Her face didn't look quite as much like a witch when she smiled.

"I like to go for walks," said Sam, reaching for a second cookie. "And also I like to ride in my stroller. I have a stroller that folds up and looks like an umbrella. You could push me in it. It has a pocket where my blanky rides. Cookies could ride there, too."

"Well," said Gertrustein, "that sounds like a good idea."

*

When they went home, Anastasia had a chipped pitcher for her mother. Sam had two cookies in his pocket and a date to go for a walk the next day.

Anastasia felt funny. She felt the same way she had when Sam was born, when her mother brought him home from the hospital, and friends came to visit to see the new baby. They brought gifts: little sweaters and stretch-suits and stuffed animals. They stood beside his crib, looking down, and said how cute he was.

Anastasia had loved him, even then, even when he was just born and only weighed eight pounds and hadn't even ever smiled at her yet. But when all those people had come and talked about how cute he was, she had gone into her own room and closed the door. She had said to Frank Goldfish, then, "Don't tell anyone this, Frank. But sometimes I hate Sam."

She had a feeling now that she wanted to go say that to Frank again. She didn't know just why.

On the way home, Sam said happily, "Gertrustein really likes me."

Anastasia smiled sweetly at him and said, "Wait till she finds out you still wear diapers, big shot."

*

At home, there was loud music playing in the living room. The Verdi Requiem. Her father had found it. He was standing in the center of the room with his eyes closed, waving his arms, holding a pencil in one hand. Anastasia giggled. She thought her father was the only person in the world who conducted orchestras that he couldn't even see.

She and Sam tiptoed past.

She found her mother in the room that the real estate lady had called the solarium. Its name had been changed, now, to the studio. Her mother was there, humming, with a pitcher — she had found their pitcher — of iced tea on a paint-spattered table. She was leaning canvases against the wall. An easel was set up.

"Hi!" she said. "How was your visit? Look! Don't you love this room?"

"Yeah," sighed Anastasia. "I see you guys have recovered from your depression. But now I've got it."

"What's wrong? Was she really a witch? I see she gave you a pitcher."

Anastasia curled up in a battered armchair. "No. She looks like a witch, Sam was right about that. But she's just an old woman with very messy hair."

"So why do you look so miserable?"

Anastasia drew patterns with her fingers on the arm of the chair. Finally she said, "She didn't like me. She only liked Sam."

Her mother kissed the top of her head. "Are you sure, sweetie? Tell me about her."

Anastasia told her all that she could.

"She sounds lonely," said her mother, sipping some iced tea thoughtfully.

"Yeah. She said all her friends were dead."

"Well, forgive me if I sound like Ann Landers for a moment. But I think I can explain something. People who are lonely have usually been disappointed by people. So they become defensive. Do you know what *defensive* means?"

"Yeah. Having weapons. Nuclear bombs. Dad's always bellowing about the defense budget."

Her mother chuckled. "Well, it's sort of the same thing. Sounds as if she has a whole arsenal over there. Her big weapon is not liking anyone. That way . . ."

". . . no one can disappoint her, right?"

"Right."

Anastasia frowned. "But she liked Sam. She *really* liked Sam," she said darkly.

"Sweetie, with all due respect to Sam, he doesn't really qualify as a mature person yet. So she can take the risk of liking him."

"But why not me? I wouldn't disappoint her. I wouldn't let her down."

"Well," said her mother decisively, "maybe you'll have to prove that to her."

Anastasia thought for a long time. "You know what I think I'll do, if Dad will drive me to the dime store?"

"What?"

"Well, someone who never ever disappoints me, and who keeps me from being lonely, is Frank. I think I'll buy Gertrustein a goldfish."

✼

Her father still had his eyes closed, so he didn't see her come into the living room. But now he had come to the part in Verdi's Requiem where he always sang along with the record. Anastasia cringed. She lived in mortal fear that someday one of her friends would be there when her father was belting out the tenor solo from the Verdi Requiem, with his eyes closed and sweat on his bald head.

Of course now that they lived in the suburbs where she didn't *have* any friends, that couldn't happen. Her depression came back.

Toward the end, at the very high part, her father stood on his tiptoes while he sang. Anastasia giggled.

He opened his eyes when it ended and bowed to Anastasia, who applauded politely; then he went and switched the stereo to Off. He wiped his damp face with his handkerchief.

"I'm always too exhausted to conduct the next section after I sing that section," he said. "How did I sound?"

"Pretty good. You're getting better, I think."

" '*Inter oves lacum praesta et ab haedis me sequestra,*' " he said. She recognized them as some of the words he had sung. "Know what that means?"

"Nope."

"You will after you study Latin. It means, 'Give me a place among the sheep and separate me from the goats.' "

Anastasia laughed. "Okay. You're among the sheep."

"So are you. In fact, I don't know anybody who is among the goats."

"I do. Gertrude Stein."

Her father put his handkerchief away and looked at her in astonishment. "Don't tell me you've become familiar with Gertrude Stein!"

"Yeah. Just today. Do you know her already?"

"*Know* her! I teach her in a graduate seminar. Gertrude Stein, Amy Lowell, Ezra Pound, and Henry James."

Anastasia wrinkled her forehead. "She's awfully *old* to be going to school still."

"No, no. She's not a student. She's a *writer*. I teach my students about her writing."

"That's funny. She didn't tell Sam and me she was a writer."

"What are you talking about? How could she tell you and Sam anything? She's dead."

Good grief. Anastasia's stomach felt funny. She's a

ghost. I'm living in a ghost story. Gertrustein is dead. No wonder she looks so awful.

"Anastasia," said her father suddenly, "I have a feeling that you and I are talking about two different Gertrude Steins."

"The one I'm talking about lives next door to us. She looks like a witch."

"Oh. Well, the one I'm talking about is dead, and she looked like a car mechanic."

Anastasia started to laugh. "If Gertrustein next door were a car mechanic, maybe she could fix our car so it wouldn't backfire."

Her father chuckled. "Maybe so. Now scoot. I want to conduct this last section of the Requiem."

"After you do that, could you drive me to the dime store? I want to buy Gertrustein a goldfish."

One of the things that Anastasia loved most about her father was that when you said something like you wanted to buy a goldfish for the next-door neighbor who looked like a witch, he didn't say "why." He said, "Okay," switched on the stereo, closed his eyes, and began to wave his arms in the air.

*

Anastasia looked again at the title she had written on the day the movers came. "The Mystery of Saying Good-by." It still seemed, as it had that day, a wonderful title. She chewed on her pencil eraser for a while.

Then she began the first paragraph of her book.

"Once there was a young girl," Anastasia wrote, "who

had had, in her short life of twelve years, to say good-by many times. Her grandmother had died. And her goldfish had been flushed down the toilet and was irretrievable even though plumbers had been called.

"She had said good-by to her grandmother two ways. One, by going to the funeral, which was okay even though it was sad. And two, by keeping her grand- mother's wedding ring, which was given to her, and look- ing at it now and then, which made her remember her grandmother in a nice sort of way.

"And she had said good-by to her goldfish by holding memorial services over the toilet bowl, and playing taps on a harmonica. Her father had sung 'Many brave hearts are asleep in the deep.'

"But one day, she had to say good-by to the house she had lived in all her life. Actually it was an apartment, but apartments can *feel* like houses, and this young girl's apartment had always felt like a house to her.

"That was the hardest good-by of all, because there was no funeral, no souvenir to keep, no memorial service, no harmonica music, no final flush.

"Also, it became complicated, because at the same time she had to adjust to a *new* house. This young girl was not a very adjustable person."

Anastasia read that again, and then she crossed out the last two sentences. She didn't like the word *adjustable*. It sounded like a training bra.

". . . she had to *adapt* to a new house. This young girl was not a very adaptable person," she wrote.

She chewed on her eraser again, and watched Frank

the Second swirl gently around his bowl. Frank hadn't even seemed to notice that he was living in the suburbs now.

She wondered if whoever published her book would mind if it had footnotes. At the end of the sentence she had just written, she made an asterisk.

Now it said, "This young girl was not a very adaptable person." *

At the bottom of the page, she wrote:

* For reasons that scientists have not yet figured out, goldfish seem to be more adaptable than young girls.

Anastasia took the new goldfish up to her tower bedroom. He (she? it was hard to tell, with goldfish) had survived the trip home from the dime store comfortably, and she set the little bowl on her desk beside Frank Goldfish's bowl.

"Frank," she said, "this is going to be your next-door neighbor."

Then she opened the little bag of goldfish things on which she had spent most of her savings.

"Frank," she said, "don't be embarrassed about all this stuff. I got it because I thought Gertrustein would probably like it. I know *you* wouldn't like it." And she put into the new goldfish bowl a handful of pink pebbles, a plastic castle, and a little fake man in a diving suit.

Frank made a face as if he had eaten a lemon.

"Yeah, I know, Frank. It's really stupid looking. But you haven't met Gertrustein. Her house is full of stuff that you and I wouldn't like. But *she* likes it, and that's what matters. And this is going to be her goldfish."

She sprinkled some fish food into both bowls and watched the two goldfish eat. She wondered if goldfish ever felt lonely. *She* was beginning to feel lonely. On the way to the dime store, she had seen some kids her age: a boy mowing a lawn a few houses away and two girls sitting together on a porch. Maybe if she walked past, she could say hi. But what if they didn't say hi back? Or what if they *did?* What would she say next?

She lay on her bed and looked around the room. Through the windows, she could see the tops of trees and a lot of sky. It was nice, being up in a tower. Vaguely she remembered the fairy tale of Rapunzel, who had been locked in a tower, and who had hung her long hair from the window so that her lover could climb up. That was kind of neat.

But then Anastasia ran her fingers through her own hair, which had begun to be pretty long — halfway down her back — but she realized that it needed washing again. Yuck. If a lover tried to climb her greasy hair, he would slide back down.

Not that she wanted a lover, anyway, for pete's sake. But a *friend* would be nice.

Her old furniture was all in this room, but the room didn't feel familiar yet. She began to wish that she hadn't thrown her orangutan poster away. And she missed her old wallpaper. She had gotten to know the funny-looking bicycle riders on her old wallpaper quite well. She had even given them names. The lady in the long skirt who rode a unicycle and played a violin was named Sibyl. The man on an old-fashioned racing bike who rode no-hands and played a flute was Stanley. Stanley had chased Sibyl around the walls of her old bedroom for years. She wanted them back.

This wallpaper was old, with dumb flowers. In some places, in the corners, it was peeling a little.

Anastasia clattered down the stairs and found her mother arranging the kitchen cupboards.

"Mom, I miss Stanley and Sybil."

Her mother frowned at a souffle dish and finally put it into the cupboard beside the refrigerator.

"Who are Stanley and Sybil? I thought you would miss Jenny MacCauley."

"I *do* miss Jenny. But I'm going to call her on the phone. Stanley and Sybil are the people on my wallpaper."

Her mother smiled. "Oh, of course. I forgot they had names. Stanley had that sexy little mustache. I'm not surprised that you miss them."

"My room doesn't feel like mine. I *like* it. But it's strange, still."

Her mother took a heavy bowl out of the packing carton. "If you were a yellow pottery bowl with squiggle designs on your sides, where would you want to live?" she asked.

Anastasia thought, and then pointed to a cupboard. "There," she said.

Her mother put the yellow bowl into that cupboard. "I have an idea," she said.

"What?" Usually her mother had pretty good ideas.

"I could find out if they still make that Stanley-and-Sibyl wallpaper. And if they do, we could have your room papered with it. We were going to wallpaper that room anyway."

Anastasia thought. "I chose that paper when I was eight. You don't think it would be dumb to still want it when I'm twelve?"

"No. It wouldn't be dumb. It was pretty grown-up paper. I remember thinking when you were eight that it was a sophisticated choice."

"No kidding?"

"No kidding."

Anastasia grinned. "Okay. I'd really like that, to have Stanley and Sibyl back."

Her mother nodded and put away a few more dishes. "I forgot to tell you something. I'm sorry. Someone named Robert called, while you were off buying the goldfish."

"*Robert* called?"

"Yes. Who's Robert?"

Anastasia groaned. "Did he have a sort of squeaky voice?"

"Well, maybe it was a little squeaky. He sounded very pleasant, though."

Good grief. It was dumb Robert Giannini. *Typical* of

that jerk Robert Giannini to sound *pleasant* to somebody's mother.

"It's a guy who was in my class at school."

"Oh. Well, he wants you to call him back. I wrote his number on that pad of paper by the phone."

Anastasia made a face. "I can't call him. What would I say?"

Her mother looked surprised. Sometimes her mother didn't understand *anything*. "You would say, 'This is Anastasia. My mother said you called while I was out.'"

Good grief. What a dumb thing to say. Anastasia made another face and wandered off to the telephone. She stared at Robert Giannini's number for a while. She already knew what it was. She had looked it up in the phone book about a hundred times. Just because she was bored. Not for any other reason.

"Robert," she said, when he answered the phone, "this is Anastasia. My mother said you called while I was out."

"Yeah. Hi. I got your number from information."

"What did you call for? Is anything interesting happening in Cambridge? Have you collected any new stuff?"

"Cambridge is the same as ever. Everything's pretty boring here. It's hot. It's even too hot to ride down to the river."

"Yeah, it's hot here, too."

"Have you made any new friends?"

"Robert, I've only lived here for three days. I haven't had time. I've only made a couple of new friends." It was

73

only a partial lie. She had met Gertrustein, anyway. And she had *seen* some kids on the block, even though she hadn't met them.

"Girls or boys?"

Good grief. Robert was the kind of person who wanted to know *details*. It was awfully hard to give details when you were telling partial lies.

"One girl and one boy," Anastasia said. "The girl is actually a woman. She lives next door. And the boy lives down the street."

Now she would have to go down the street to where the boy was mowing the lawn and introduce herself. Then it wouldn't be a lie at all.

"Oh," said Robert. "How old is the boy?"

"I don't know. About thirteen or fourteen, I think."

"Oh." Robert didn't say anything else for a minute. Finally he said, "Guess what, Anastasia. I invented a system to tell the future."

Now *that* was interesting. All her life, Anastasia had wanted to be able to know about the future. The horoscopes in magazines and newspapers weren't good enough. They never gave details. But if Robert Giannini, the Detail Freak, had invented a system — well, that could be interesting. Anastasia sat down on the floor.

"Tell me about it," she said.

"You need a pencil and paper."

"I have some right here."

"Okay. First, write down the alphabet, and then write down numbers by the letters. 1 is A, and 2 is B. Like that, all the way through the alphabet. Z is 26."

That was easy enough. Anastasia did it on a piece of paper. "Okay," she said, when she was finished.

"All right. Now here's what you do. I'll tell you how I did mine and how it came out. First you write down your age. I'm 12, so I wrote down 12."

"Okay. I'm 12, too." She wrote it down.

"Then you write down the day of the month your birthday is on. Mine's September 20th, so I wrote down 20."

"Mine's 9. October 9th."

"Now add those together. Next you add today's date."

"What's today?"

"The 16th. Add 16."

"Okay."

"Now add your favorite TV channel. Mine's 5."

"Mine's 56. I like the old movies on Channel 56."

"Okay, add 56."

"Then what?"

"This is the last one. You add the last three numbers of your phone number. Mine are 058."

"I know," Anastasia said. "I just dialed them."

"Now," said Robert triumphantly. "Look at the number you end up with — and then look at the alphabet. There's your future!"

"I don't understand."

"I came out with 111. So look at letter 1 and letter 11. A and K. Your initials, Anastasia!"

Anastasia made a face. "You're weird, Robert."

"What number did you get?"

Anastasia checked her addition. "370." She looked at

the alphabet. "C and G. Big deal. I don't know a single person with those initials. Unless Clark Gable is going to come back from the grave."

There was a silence. "Well, maybe if you liked some other TV channel. Walt Disney's on Channel 4 on Sunday nights. Don't you like Walt Disney?"

"Yuck. Robert, this is really a dumb system you invented."

"Well, it worked for *me*." She could tell from Robert's voice that he was mad.

"I'll do it again tomorrow when the date is different. Maybe by tomorrow I'll like a different TV channel, too."

"Okay," Robert muttered.

"I have to go now, Robert."

"I might ride my bike out to see you. I looked on the map, and it's not too far."

"Okay," said Anastasia. "But call first. Because I might be busy with my new friends or something."

She felt like a rotten person after she hung up. But honestly. Robert was such a jerk. Your age. The date. Your favorite TV channel. Your phone number. All of those things *change*, for pete's sake. How could anybody know anything about the future *ever*, when everything changes all the time?

Anyway, she thought suddenly, if you *did* know the future, there wouldn't be any *surprises* left.

Back in the kitchen, her parents were measuring the windows so that her mother could make curtains.

Once, several years ago, her parents had had a huge fight about sewing. Anastasia's mother had suddenly said, one day, that she didn't see why she automatically did all the mending and sewing. She was sewing some buttons onto something at the time and had just pricked her finger with the needle, and she had the tip of her finger in her mouth, sucking it, when suddenly she got mad.

"This is the most sexist household in Cambridge," she had announced angrily. "Why is it that the wife gets stuck with the sewing? Myron, you do some of the *cooking*. Will you tell me one good reason why you don't *sew?*"

"Because I don't know how," Dr. Krupnik had said, chewing on his pipe.

"I'll teach you, then."

"Thank you, but I don't *want* to know how to sew."

Her mother sat there for a minute, sucking her finger, looking madder and madder. "In that case," she said, finally, "thank you, but I don't want to do any laundry anymore. Ever."

"In *that* case," said her father, "I don't think I want to be an English professor anymore. I have always, if you must know, wanted to be a beachcomber. So I think that from now on I will walk on empty beaches — all alone, by the way — and recite poetry to myself. Of course that means that there will be no more paychecks."

Anastasia's mother folded the shirt which was still missing two buttons, very neatly, and laid it on the table. "As a matter of fact, *I* have been wanting for a long time to go to the Cotswolds and live in a small cottage with a thatched roof — all alone, by the way — and paint."

77

Anastasia had scurried away to her room, terrified. If her father became a beachcomber — all alone — and her mother went to the Cotswolds, whatever the Cotswolds were — all alone — what would happen to Anastasia?

But after a while, she heard her parents laughing. When she went back to where they were, her mother was giggling and had her father's pipe in her mouth, and her father was sewing a button on his shirt.

Since then, her mother had always done all the sewing. Anastasia couldn't figure it out. It was something like item number 124 in her list of things she absolutely didn't understand.

Now her mother was about to make curtains for the kitchen. The fabric, bright blue with yellow and orange suns and moons and stars all over it, was unfolded on the kitchen table.

"Those curtains are going to be weird," Anastasia said cheerfully.

Her father turned, with a tape measure dangling around his neck, and said loudly, "That's *it*."

"*What's* it, Dad?"

"That word. Weird. I have heard you use the word *weird* at least four thousand times in the past week."

"But . . ."

"Anastasia, this is a household of verbal, articulate, intelligent people. We have an entire room filled with bookcases. In those bookcases there are dictionaries. Encyclopedias. *Roget's Thesaurus*. Anthologies of obscure Elizabethan poetry. There are a *hundred* words — at *least* a hundred words — that you could substitute for *weird*."

"Name some."

He got a beer from the refrigerator. "*Strange*," he said. "*Dreadful. Formidable. Ghastly. Unearthly. Demoniacal . . .*"

Anastasia could tell, when he got to *demoniacal*, that he was going to go on for quite a while. She grabbed a cookie and began to back out of the room.

"I'm going to take Gertrustein her goldfish," she muttered.

"*PHANTASMAGORICAL!*" said her father, and took another gulp of beer.

Anastasia closed the door quietly. Sam appeared on the stairs with wet diapers and rosy cheeks, coming down from his room after his nap. "What's the matter with Daddy?" he asked.

Anastasia shrugged and gave Sam half of her cookie. "He's being weird," she said.

*

"Frank, I'm going to take your buddy next door. I hope you won't miss him too much," said Anastasia. But Frank kissed the side of his bowl and wiggled his behind. He didn't mind.

Her novel in her notebook was open on her desk. Anastasia picked up her pencil and read what she had written so far, concluding with the footnote. It seemed enough for Chapter 1.

"Chapter 2," she wrote on the next page.

"The young girl decided," she wrote, "that one way to adapt to a new house was to make friends. And one way to make friends was to take them a gift.

"A lot of people find that food is a good gift to take to someone. Sometimes people make an apple pie, or a macaroni and cheese casserole, and they take it next door to their neighbors, and after that they are friends.

"But the young girl didn't know how to cook . . ."

Then she crossed that out. It was a novel, after all. It didn't have to be the complete truth.

"But the young girl didn't care much for cooking, although she was very good at it. Also, it was ninety degrees outside, and too hot to turn on the stove. So she decided to take her next-door neighbor a fish. It was not a *cooked* fish."

She read over what she had written, and it didn't sound just right. Anastasia scowled and tore the whole page out. Good grief: it was really *hard* to write a novel, even after you had a good title.

It was not easy to push the doorbell without spilling the goldfish bowl, but after a moment Anastasia managed a good shrill ring. After another moment, she could hear Gertrustein's shuffling footsteps and then her voice: "Who's there?"

"It's Anastasia again."

The door opened, and Gertrustein peered out. "Anastasia Again? It looks like Anastasia Krupnik to me! Hah!" The "hah" was a hiccuppy sort of laugh, which was more of a laugh than her dumb joke deserved, Anastasia thought.

"I brought you something. A goldfish."

Gertrustein looked at the goldfish and the goldfish bowl for a moment. Then she nodded and invited Anastasia inside. That was a relief. Anastasia had thought that she would have to *explain* about the goldfish. I guess when you get old, she thought, you get over being surprised by stuff. So when someone brings you a goldfish, you don't even ask why.

They put the goldfish bowl on a table in the living room next to a plastic vase of artificial flowers. Gertrustein leaned close to the bowl and watched intently as the fish swam in circles, flipping his tail. The little diver stood on the bottom of the bowl, tilted slightly, wearing his huge plastic helmet.

Suddenly Gertrustein began to laugh. Anastasia thought that was rude, to begin to laugh at a gift before you had even said thank you.

"What are you going to name your goldfish?" asked Anastasia politely, pretending not to notice that Gertrustein was laughing.

But she just laughed harder.

"My goldfish is named Frank," said Anastasia. "I don't know if yours is male or female, though."

Gertrustein looked at her, still chuckling. "It's male, of course. It's the funniest thing I've ever seen. I'll name him Mr. Stein. He looks exactly like my husband. The same popeyes."

Anastasia glanced around the room for signs of a husband. At her house, there were always pipes lying in ashtrays or size-twelve sneakers in a corner. But there was no indication of a Mr. Stein.

"Where *is* your husband?" she asked.

"Oh, goodness. I haven't any idea. He's been gone for

forty years. He ran off with a lady mandolin player who wore bright blue shoes."

"Well," said Anastasia uneasily, "I'm very sorry he did that."

But Gertrustein was laughing again. "Oh, don't be. He looked like a goldfish, although I never realized it until this afternoon. I was *glad* when he ran off. I never should have married him."

"Why did you, then?"

"I was a spinster. Do you know what a spinster is?"

"Yeah. I think I'm going to be one, because I'm so tall, and everything. Boys don't like me, except one boy, and I don't like *him*."

"Nonsense. Give yourself time. How old are you?"

"Twelve."

"Well, I was over *thirty,* and not married. Lived right in this house, the same house where I had been born. Lived here all alone because my parents were both dead by then. And along came Mr. Stein one day, selling cookware door to door . . ."

"Did you buy any?"

"Bought the whole batch. Still have it. It outlasted Mr. Stein."

"Excuse me, but why do you call him Mr. Stein? My mother calls my father Myron."

Gertrustein began to laugh so hard that the sofa on which they were sitting wiggled.

"His name was Lloyd," she sputtered. "Lloyd Stein. But I'll have to tell you what happened on our wedding night . . ."

Good grief. Anastasia liked reading about people's wedding nights in *Cosmopolitan* magazine or in Gothic novels. But she certainly didn't want to hear about a *real person's* wedding night.

Gertrustein took a deep breath so that she would stop laughing. Then she said, "The night that we were married, Mr. Stein said to me, 'Gertrude, are you familiar with the word which is spelled L-L-A-M-A?' I thought for a moment, and then I said, 'Of course. Llama. It's an animal with a sad, smiling sort of face.'"

Anastasia nodded. It was the same way she would have described a llama.

"Then he said, 'Gertrude, your description is correct, but your pronunciation is wrong. When a word begins with a double L, the double L is pronounced as Y. Therefore the correct way to say *llama* is, in fact *yama*, don't you see? Very few people know that,' he said. 'Well,' I told him, 'I certainly never knew that.'"

"I didn't either," said Anastasia.

"Then he told me, 'So you can see, of course, that the correct pronunciation of *Lloyd* is, actually, *Yoyd*. I would prefer that you pronounce my name correctly, now that we are man and wife. Please call me Yoyd from now on.'"

"Good grief," said Anastasia, beginning to giggle.

"Good grief indeed. How on earth can you call someone *Yoyd*? I wanted to hit him over his silly, pompous, popeyed head with one of the aluminum saucepans that he had sold me. I didn't, of course. But you can see that it was somewhat fortunate that the mandolin player came along. In three years I had never called him by name. He hated laughter. And I could never have said Yoyd without laughing. When I had to speak to him at all, I called him Mr. Stein."

"A magazine that I read a lot would call that a Brief and Unfortunate Marriage."

"Yes. It was certainly a Brief and Unfortunate Marriage."

"Did you ever look up *llama* in the dictionary? To see if maybe he was right?"

"Of course not. Of course he wasn't right. He was an idiot with goldfish eyes."

"Well, I'm sorry that you married him."

"Me too. But it was understandable, I guess. I was over thirty, after all, and all alone. I liked his aluminum cookware. And the man I loved had married someone else."

Now *that* was romantic and interesting.

"What was *his* name?"

Gertrustein looked a little bit sad. "Edward Evans. We had grown up together. As a matter of fact, Anastasia, Edward lived in your house, when he was a boy."

It was always hard to imagine old people being *young*. Anastasia looked for a long time at Gertrustein and just couldn't see even the smallest fragments of a young face. Sam had been right; she really did look like a witch.

"I don't mean to be rude or anything," Anastasia said, "but you know, Gertrustein, you really would look much nicer if you would fix your hair differently."

Gertrustein held up her hands. They were twisted and

misshapen. "It's all I can do to hold a hairbrush," she explained. "My arthritis is so bad."

"Well," said Anastasia, "tomorrow, when you take Sam for a walk, why don't you walk down past the drugstore? And buy some curlers, and when you come back, *I'll* fix your hair for you!"

Gertrustein thought about that, frowning. "All right," she said, finally. "We'll give it a try, now that there is a new Mr. Stein in the house."

In his bowl, the new Mr. Stein gazed out with bulging eyes, swished his tail, and swooped around the plastic diver. Anastasia, who was an expert on goldfish emotions, could tell that he was quite happy.

❖

"Mom, I have something important to talk to you about."

"How do you like the curtains so far?"

One of the new curtains was hanging at one window. The others were still spread out on the kitchen table beside the sewing machine.

"Fine. They look pretty good. Can you stop sewing for a minute?"

"Sure. What's on your mind?"

Anastasia sat down on one of the kitchen chairs, opposite her mother, and wrapped her feet around the rungs. "This is sort of embarrassing," she said. "Promise you won't tell anyone."

"Okay. I promise."

"Well, I feel sort of weird about this. I'm sorry, but

there isn't any word except weird for it. But I think I'm going to have to marry Robert Giannini."

Anastasia had always thought that it was only in books that people's mouths fell open in surprise. But her mother's mouth fell open in surprise.

"Anastasia! That's *impossible!* How could that be? You're only twelve years old! You can't possibly . . ."

"Mom," Anastasia said impatiently. "I didn't mean *now*. I mean *years* from now, after I finish college. But I might as well start getting used to the idea now. And that's what makes me feel weird. Because I can't *stand* Robert Giannini. I had sort of decided that maybe I could learn to like him, because I do like him a little bit sometimes. But I was just talking to Gertrustein, and she was telling me how she married someone she couldn't stand, although she liked his aluminum cookware, but she never did learn to like him, because he wanted her to call him Yoyd, and then he ran off with a mandolin player, and . . ."

"Hold on. Hold everything. I very rarely want a beer in the middle of the afternoon. But suddenly I want a beer. Can I get you something?"

"Are there any Popsicles?"

Her mother came back from the refrigerator with a can of beer and a green Popsicle. Anastasia peeled off the paper and began to lick the Popsicle carefully.

"Now, for starters. Why do you think you're going to have to marry Robert Giannini in ten or fifteen years?"

"Because he loves me. And he's the only boy who ever

has or ever will. Now don't feel bad about this, Mom, because it isn't your fault, but I *am* a sort of freak. In fifth grade I was the tallest girl in the class, but the boys were taller, most of them. But in sixth grade I was the tallest *person* in the class. There weren't any boys as tall as me, and I was even taller than the teacher. By the time I finish high school, I will probably be one of the world's tallest human beings. I also have the world's most hideous hair, in case you haven't noticed.

"Now for some reason Robert Giannini doesn't seem to mind what I look like. He's the only male in the world who will ever feel that way, so probably I'm lucky to have found him. The trouble is, I think *he's* revolting. I hate his squeaky voice. And I hate it that he carries a dumb briefcase everywhere. I can't *stand* it that he wears a SeaWorld tee shirt. But I have to figure out how to adjust to those things if I'm going to marry him, because I certainly don't want to have a Brief and Unfortunate Marriage, for pete's sake ..."

"Whoa. You're going much too fast for me, Anastasia. Wait a minute." Her mother sipped at the beer and looked puzzled. "First of all, what makes you so sure you want to get married at all? Lots of women never do and are perfectly happy."

"Would you be?"

"No, I like being married. But that doesn't mean that *you* have to."

Anastasia sucked on her Popsicle and thought for a long time. She thought about the time that her mother had had the flu and her father had taken cups of tea to her and sat beside her bed, not minding that he might catch the flu, too.

Then she thought about what it would be like to be in bed with the flu if there were no one to bring cups of tea and sit beside your bed. It made her feel lonely, just thinking about it.

Then she thought about the day that Sam was born, and her father took her mother to the hospital and stayed there with her while Sam was being born, and when he came home, he was so excited that he couldn't remember if the baby weighed eight pounds and four ounces or four pounds and eight ounces; and she and her father smoked cigars to celebrate, only hers was a chocolate cigar.

She thought about what it would be like to have a baby if you weren't married, and nobody stayed with you while the baby was being born and smoked a cigar afterward to celebrate. It made her feel lonely.

She thought about not ever having a baby at all. That made her feel even lonelier.

"I really do want to get married someday," she said, finally.

"Okay," said her mother. "First of all, then, about Robert. I've never met him, but I'll take your word for it that some things about him right now are revolting. But he's how old? Twelve?"

"Yeah."

"Well, I didn't know your dad when he was twelve. But I'll bet you anything he had a squeaky voice. Robert's voice will change. He'll grow taller. And I can guarantee you that within the next year, his mother will be using the SeaWorld tee shirt as a cleaning rag. Do you know what I was using as a cleaning rag just this very morning?"

"What?"

"A pink tee shirt with ruffles on the neck and daisies embroidered on the sleeves."

"Oh, *gross*. I'd forgotten that shirt."

"Well, you loved it when you were eight or nine. People's tastes change. Robert's will, too."

"Yeah, probably he won't even like *me* after a while." Anastasia caught the last piece of green Popsicle just before it slid off the stick. She fired the empty stick into the wastebasket with a long, arching basketball shot.

Her mother laughed. "Well, maybe not. But other boys will."

"Hah," said Anastasia gloomily.

"Hah. Trust me. I promise you that will be true. Did you just hear something? I thought I heard a buzzer."

"The doorbell. It's the first time anyone has rung the doorbell since we moved in! I'll get it."

The boy at the front door was the same boy that Anastasia had seen mowing a lawn down the street. She had walked past him twice, trying to get up the nerve to say hi. Now he was standing right here on the front porch, looking at her. He was looking *down* at her, because he was a little taller than she, and he was wearing cut-off jeans and a rugby shirt. He looked a little like Luke Skywalker. When he said hi, she noticed his voice was a little squeaky, like Robert's.

His voice will change, she thought happily.

"Hi," she said.

"My name's Steve Harvey. I live down the street, and I saw that you guys moved in, and I wondered if you wanted your lawn mowed. I've got my lawn mower right outside."

"Well, I'll ask my mother, but I'm absolutely certain she'll say yes. She was just saying this morning that the grass needed to be cut." What she had said, actually, at breakfast, was, "Myron, we have to buy a lawn mower and cut this grass."

"My name is Anastasia Krupnik," she added, before she went to get her mother.

"What grade are you in?"

"I'll be in seventh."

"Me too. You'll probably be in my homeroom because they do it alphabetically."

"Oh. Well, it'll be nice to know someone in my homeroom before I start school."

"Yeah. It's lousy to be the new kid. I know, because I just moved here last year. But it doesn't take long to make friends. Do you play tennis?"

"Not very well."

"Me neither. But there are courts down behind the school. You want to play later?"

"Sure. Wait here a minute, and I'll go ask my mom about the lawn."

Her mother was standing in the kitchen, grinning.

"Mom, there's a boy at the door who . . ."

"I know. I was eavesdropping."

"We *do* need the grass cut. You were just saying to Dad this morning that..."

"Anastasia, up in my bathroom there's a brand new bottle of shampoo. You'll have time to wash your hair and dry it while he's doing the lawn."

"Do you think maybe I should shave my legs?" whispered Anastasia.

"The last time you tried to shave your legs," her mother whispered back, "you practically needed blood transfusions. I'd forget it if I were you."

"*Cosmopolitan* magazine says that it's fashionable not to, especially if you have blonde hair, like me."

"Fine. Wonderful. Now scoot. I'll get him started on the lawn."

✦

Hmmm, thought Anastasia, as her hair dried, and she practiced her backhand, standing in the center of her tower bedroom. Maybe it's true, what Mom said. Maybe other boys besides Robert Giannini will like me.'

Maybe *this* boy will.

Maybe my hair will look okay when I go to play tennis.

Maybe my legs aren't quite as skinny as they were last month.

Maybe I will think of something intelligent to say to him. And maybe I won't hit the ball into the net every time, the way I usually do.

I think I will have a hyphenated name, she thought, when I get married. Anastasia Krupnik-Harvey, she thought. That doesn't sound too bad.

Anastasia peeled a strip of the old, loosened, flowered wallpaper from the wall of her room, exposing an even older layer of paper underneath. She rolled the strip into a ball and shot it into the wastebasket.

Outside, she could hear the clatter of Steve Harvey's lawn mower.

Maybe I will get to feeling at home in this room before too long, she thought.

Maybe the suburbs aren't as bad as I used to think.

Maybe I was making premature assumptions.

Anastasia picked up her notebook and began a new version of Chapter 2.

"After she moved to her new home," Anastasia wrote, "the young girl began to be more adaptable than she had been in the past. She began to take up tennis, as a hobby."

The phone rang, and it was Jenny MacCauley.

"Jenny! I've called you twice, and you weren't home either time."

"Oh. I guess I was out."

"Yeah, your mother said you were out. How are things in Cambridge?"

"Booorrring," said Jenny mournfully.

"Yeah, here too. Booorrring," said Anastasia.

"Do you hate it there?"

"Well, sort of," Anastasia lied. "When are you going to come see me?"

"I thought Robert and I might ride our bikes out next Saturday. He said he looked at a map and figured out how to get there."

"Robert *Giannini?* When did you talk to *him?*"

Jenny hesitated. "Well, yesterday he came over and we rode our bikes down to the river."

"That jerk."

"Yeah, that jerk Giannini. Anyway, we sat by the river for a while because Robert was doing one of his surveys. We were counting joggers. How many old joggers and how many young. How many male and how many female. How many wearing special jogging shoes. How many female joggers wearing bras and how many not. Robert's going to send the results of his survey to *Psychology Today*."

"That idiot."

"Yeah. Anyway, after that we went over to the Brattle Theater and saw *Casablanca*."

"JENNY MACCAULEY! YOU TOLD ME THAT WE WOULD GO SEE THAT TOGETHER. YOU KNOW I'VE ONLY EVER SEEN IT ON TV!"

"Well, you weren't *here*, Anastasia."

Anastasia glowered. "Funny that you said things were boring in Cambridge, Jenny. It sure doesn't *sound* boring."

There was a long silence. Finally Jenny changed the subject. "Have you met anyone out there?"

"Yeah. The woman next door. She takes Sam out for a walk every afternoon."

"Any boys?"

"Yes, as a matter of fact. A boy named Steve Harvey. He's going to be in the seventh grade, and he's tall and good-looking. I've played tennis with him three after-noons now."

Jenny interrupted her. "You're a terrible tennis player. You always hit the ball into the net."

"That's because I never had a good partner before, Jenny MacCauley, you rat," said Anastasia angrily. "It just so happens that when I play tennis with Steve Harvey, I hit the ball over the net at least fifty per cent of the time. We're playing again today. Probably by the end of the week I'll hit the ball over the net *eighty* per cent of the time, and probably —"

Jenny interrupted her again. "Anastasia," she said pointedly, "you promised me you'd *call* me if you met any boys."

"I *did* call you. You were always *out*. You were always out seeing *Casablanca* with Robert Giannini, probably."

"So? You're always out, playing tennis, it sounds like. Funny that you said things were boring *there*."

There was another long and uncomfortable silence.

"Are people like you expected in the suburbs?" asked Jenny finally. "Do they wear pink curlers and eat TV dinners and have bowls of artificial fruit?"

Anastasia thought about the past three afternoons, when she had gone to Gertrustein's house after tennis and rolled Gertrustein's ragged gray hair up in pink curlers so that she would look nicer. On one of those days, Gertrustein had put a TV dinner into the oven while Anastasia was there. She had explained how she very seldom did much cooking anymore, because it was so lonely to cook for just one person.

"Yeah," said Anastasia to Jenny. "The lady next door is just like that. Pink curlers. TV dinners. Artificial fruit. The whole bit."

"Sick-o," said Jenny.

"Yeah," said Anastasia vaguely. "I guess."

"Listen, I gotta go. But Robert and I'll ride out next Saturday, okay?"

"Okay. Hey, did Robert ask you anything about Sam? Did he say anything about Sam, well, not having any legs, or anything like that?"

"Good grief. Why would he ask me that? Sam has *legs*. He kicked me once, because I hid his blanket as a joke."

"Oh," sighed Anastasia, "it's too complicated to explain. I'll see you guys on Saturday."

"Don't forget to watch TV tonight. *The Maltese Falcon* is on."

After Anastasia had hung up, she thought, I should have asked her if she was going to watch it on TV. Or if she was going to go see it at the Brattle Theater. With Robert Giannini, that jerk.

She decided that maybe this afternoon she would get the tennis ball over the net more easily, and *harder*, by pretending that it was Robert Giannini's head. Whammo.

❀

One of the things that Anastasia liked about her tower room was that her parents didn't very often come up to it. So it was very private.

Not that she ever did anything subversive in her room. A lot of kids she knew sometimes smoked cigarettes in their rooms and then sprayed air freshener around so their parents wouldn't know; but Anastasia thought smoking cigarettes was gross.

And some kids she knew occasionally drank beer in their rooms. But there was always beer in the Krupniks' refrigerator, and whenever her father drank a beer, he gave it to her first, so that she could sip off the foam, because he didn't like foam. So she was actually pretty bored with beer, and it never seemed like a big deal, the way it did to some kids.

And of course lots of kids read dirty books in their rooms and hid them under the mattresses. But Anastasia's house had always been filled with books, and some of them had sex in them, and she had always been allowed to read whatever she wanted. Anastasia thought that dirty books were generally not as gross as cigarettes, but rather like beer: interesting now and then, in small doses, but no big deal.

So there was not, really, anything private in her room except her private notebook, and she didn't even need to hide that. Her parents had told her once that they would never read her private notebook. So she had tested them a few times, by leaving it around the house conspicuously, with an almost-invisible hair on it, which would be dislodged if anyone opened the notebook. She had learned that trick from spy novels. But the hair always remained in place. Her parents really *hadn't* opened it. Sam had, once, and scribbled with crayons on a few pages. But Sam couldn't read yet.

Still, even though she didn't need a private place for

subversive stuff, she did like having a room that was very private. It was quiet. It was a good place to read, or to think, or to daydream, or to be sad.

Right now she was lying on her bed, wondering what to do next Saturday when Robert Giannini showed up in the suburbs.

First of all, it was a problem because she didn't want Steve Harvey to know that the Other Man in her life carried an idiotic briefcase everywhere and wore a Sea-World tee shirt.

It was okay for Steve Harvey to know that there *was* an Other Man. In fact, it was probably a good thing. It made her seem *desirable*, at least, and according to *Cosmopolitan*, that was a good thing. "Keeping Him on His Toes" was the title of the article that had pointed that out.

But keeping Steve Harvey on his toes was one thing; keeping him doubled over, laughing, when he *saw* Robert Giannini was something else again.

She reached out and peeled another strip of old wallpaper from the wall, while she thought. Her wastebasket was almost full of crumpled bits of old wallpaper.

Second — Anastasia almost groaned aloud — was the problem of what to do about Sam, when Robert Giannini came. Probably that jerk was going to show up with a get-well card and a March of Dimes contribution for Anastasia's poor crippled, deformed brother.

Downstairs, she could hear the familiar padding sound which was Sam wandering around the big house in his little red sneakers. On his two very sturdy, healthy legs.

Maybe she could just shut him in his room while Robert was visiting. But that wouldn't work, she knew. Sam never stayed anyplace where you put him. He was always popping out of doors, doing his Ed MacMahon imitation. "Heeeeeere's Johnny!" Sam would announce loudly and wait for applause.

Maybe if she fed him a lot of beer, he would just go to sleep for a long time. But Sam didn't *like* beer. He didn't even like foam. It made him sneeze.

Maybe she could convince him to just sit in his stroller with a blanket over his legs. But it was ninety degrees outside. Nobody in his right mind would sit in a stroller with a blanket over his legs when it was ninety degrees.

Anastasia sighed and pulled off another strip of wallpaper. There were three layers of wallpaper. After she pulled off a piece of the top layer, she could see green flowered paper underneath. If she picked at that and peeled it off, there was a blue striped paper under that. Finally, behind the blue striped paper, there was bare plaster. It made kind of interesting designs, as she poked and peeled at the three layers.

"Anastasia? You up there? May I come up?" It was her mother calling.

"Sure. Come on up."

Her mother appeared in her room, puffing from two flights of stairs, but grinning. "Guess what! They still make Stanley and Sibyl! I've just been to the wallpaper store."

"No kidding!"

"No kidding. It costs more than it used to, but that's

okay. I ordered three rolls, and it'll be in next week. We'll have to strip off the old stuff. Oh, I see you've already started!"

"Yeah, I was just lying here thinking, and I was kind of peeling while I was thinking."

"I like to have something to do with my hands, too, while I'm thinking. Usually I knit. But I can see where peeling wallpaper would be okay, too." Her mother picked at a corner and pulled back a strip of the top layer. "What are you thinking about?"

One of the good things about Anastasia's mother was that she never laughed at you. Especially not at your problems. Anastasia always imagined Dear Abby bent double most of the day, laughing at people's problems and having to bite her tongue in order to keep a straight face while she wrote what sounded like a very serious answer.

But her mother was definitely not like that.

"I have a dumb problem," she said to her mother gloomily. "It's about Sam."

"About Sam? Has he been coloring in your notebook again? Or poking at Frank Goldfish? It's been at least six months since he's flushed anything down the toilet — I think the last time was my silver earrings, and that was just after Christmas . . ."

"No, no. It isn't anything that Sam has done. It's that . . . well, you know how weird Sam is."

"Not *weird*, Anastasia. Unusual, maybe. Precocious."

Anastasia groaned. "Well, anyway, when we were still living in Cambridge before we moved, I was talking to

Robert Giannini — who really *is* weird, by the way, I'm sorry, but there isn't any other word for Robert Giannini — and he asked me how my brother was. He's never seen Sam. And I was trying to describe Sam to Robert Giannini. And somehow, I haven't figured out how, I *never* will figure out *how*, Robert got the idea that Sam was deformed . . ."

"Deformed? *Sam?*"

"Yeah. It was because I was trying to explain how Sam grew at different rates, because that's what Dad told me, that his brain developed faster than some other parts of him. That's *true*, Mom. You know he talks like Einstein, but he still sucks his thumb and wears diapers . . ."

"Yes, but that's not *deformed*, Anastasia."

"I know that, and you know that. But for some reason Robert Giannini got the idea that poor old Sam is crippled . . ."

"Handicapped," corrected her mother.

"Okay, handicapped. And he started being very sad about it and telling me about his retarded cousin and asking if we had taken Sam to Children's Hospital and telling me about the March of Dimes . . ."

"Good grief."

"Mom, you know what? Robert Giannini was making premature assumptions."

"And you were letting him, Anastasia."

Anastasia sighed. "I know. But I don't know how it happened. And now, guess what."

"I'm not sure I want to guess what. You mean there's *more?*"

"Mom, Robert Giannini is going to ride his bike out here next Saturday."

Her mother groaned.

It was at this point, Anastasia was quite sure, that Dear Abby would take a deep breath in order to stop laughing and would write: "Dear Confused, It is very simple to solve this ridiculous problem. You must simply explain to your friend that it was a matter of poor communication, of misunderstanding, of premature assumptions. Tell him the truth about your brother. A real friend will understand."

But Anastasia's mother didn't say any of that. She didn't laugh. She just groaned.

"You want to hear a story about a terrible thing I did once?" she asked, looking embarrassed.

"Yeah." For some reason, when you had done something stupid, it always made you feel better to hear about stupid things that other people had done.

"Well, do you remember what my name was before I got married?"

"Sure. Katherine Klein."

"Well. When I was in art school, when I was oh, maybe nineteen, I had a terrific crush on a guy in one of my classes. One evening he asked me to go out and have a cup of coffee with him.

"Now, do you know that little framed print that's hanging in the hall, near the telephone? The one that's black and white, very abstract?"

"Sure. It looks like an ink blot. Like a psychiatrist would ask you what you see in it."

"Well, that's a copy of a painting by Franz Kline."

"Is he related to you?"

"No. That's the point. The name isn't even spelled the same. But Franz Kline was a very, very well-known expressionist painter. Now, we were all young art students, and we used to sit around talking for hours about painters. That's what this boy and I did that night. And somehow, in the course of the evening, he got the idea that I was Franz Kline's daughter."

"*Mom!* You didn't tell him that, did you?"

"Of course not. I just let him make the assumption. But I also didn't tell him that my father was Joseph Klein, insurance man, from Hartford, Connecticut. By the end of the evening, this boy thought that my home was in a loft in New York City, with my famous painter father."

"Good grief."

"Good grief is right. Because — as you know — there's a point at which you can say, 'Hey, no, you got it wrong.' But if you don't say it *then,* it gets harder and harder to say it, and you get in deeper and deeper."

"Did he ever find out the truth? *Did he ever come visit you at your house?*"

"No. He kept wanting to. He kept hinting that he wanted to, because of course he wanted to meet my father, or who he thought was my father. I kept making excuses."

"What happened?"

Anastasia's mother groaned, remembering. "Well, one thing that happened was that I flunked an important exam. Franz Kline *died* that year. It was in the *New York Times,* of course. So for two days I had to hide. I couldn't go to any classes — and missed an exam, so I got a failing grade — because of course I wanted this boy to think that I had gone home to the funeral and everything."

"That's *terrible.*"

"Of course it's terrible. And it's something like your situation right now. What are you going to do when Robert comes next Saturday?"

"I don't know."

"Maybe we could talk Sam into lying in bed all day with a blanket over him."

"It's too hot. I already thought of that."

"*I* know."

"What?"

"Simple. Mrs. Stein and Sam really get along very well. I'll ask her if she can babysit on Saturday. Sam can go to her house for the day. But listen, Anastasia . . ."

"What?"

"Robert Giannini's not going to come visit *often,* is he?"

"No. Absolutely not. This is the last time. I can't stand him."

❋

"Unfortunately," continued Anastasia in Chapter 2 of her novel, "just as the young girl began to live a new and well-adapted life, her past crimes began to catch up with her."

Then she crossed out the word *crimes.*

". . . her past sins began to catch up with her," she wrote.

Then she crossed out the word *sins* and chewed on her pencil eraser.

Finally she wrote, ". . . her Past began to catch up with her, and to get tangled up with her Future."

10

"It's Anastasia again," Anastasia called, after she had rung Gertrustein's doorbell. "I've brought you something!"

"Hello there, Anastasia Again," said Gertrustein, when she opened the door. It was amazing how Gertrustein's disposition had changed in a short time. Anastasia remembered how grouchy she had been, the first time they had met. Now she answered the door cheerfully, always smiling.

It had to do with her hair, thought Anastasia. Now that her hair looked pretty, Gertrustein felt cheerful. Anastasia had noticed that she *herself* felt more cheerful now that she was washing her own hair twice a day with special shampoo for oily hair. She had been doing it ever since she had met Steve Harvey. The better her hair looked, the better she felt.

Now *that* was something worth sending into *Psychol ogy Today,* instead of a dumb Giannini survey on joggers.

She would have to figure out, though, how people like her father figured into her theory. Her father was almost always cheerful even though he was bald.

"Hey, Mr. Stein is getting fat!" Anastasia peered into the goldfish bowl at the plump goldfish who stared back at her silently.

Gertrustein laughed. "I know. I think I'm feeding him too much. It's so nice to have someone to *feed* that I get carried away sometimes."

"Gertrustein," said Anastasia very seriously. "You absolutely have to make an effort to make some friends. You could invite friends over for dinner, or you could go to their house for dinner. It's not healthy to stay all shut up in your house, feeding too much to a goldfish."

But Gertrustein got a very stubborn look on her face. "I do not like people," she said, with dignity.

"Ridiculous. You're only pretending that because you're *scared* of them."

"What are you, some kind of *social worker?*"

"No. But I know what I'm talking about. Because look at me: when I moved here, I pretended that I wasn't going to like anyone in the suburbs. You know why? Because I was scared they wouldn't like *me!* And then I met you, and you like me . . . you do like me, don't you?"

"Yes," said Gertrustein reluctantly.

"And then I met Steve, and Steve likes me, at least I

think he does. And now I can't wait to meet more people. Steve's going to have a cookout at his house, and invite a lot of kids my age, and I'm really looking forward to it. It was all my imagination, that I didn't like people in the suburbs. And it's all *your* imagination, Gertrustein, and what you should do is . . ."

"You said you brought me something. What is it?" Gertrustein changed the subject.

"Oh, I almost forgot. Look!" Anastasia held up a piece of paper. "A gift certificate!"

Gertrustein took the paper and frowned at it.

"A lady came to the house," Anastasia explained, "to welcome my mother to town. She brought lots of free stuff that the town gives to new people. Two free passes to the movies — Steve and I are going to use those — and, let's see, my father gets a free oil change for the car at some gas station, and my mom gets a discount on a leg of lamb at the supermarket. We get dinner for four at some restaurant, if we go on a Tuesday night. And then there was this one, which Mom said I could give you, because she and I don't need it: a free permanent at the Clip 'n Curl Beauty Salon! If you get a permanent, your hair will look nice all the time, without my helping you put it in rollers."

Gertrustein looked dubious. "Well . . ." she said.

"Hah. I *knew* you'd say that. So I already called and made an appointment for you at the Clip 'n Curl. It's right next to the drugstore, close enough for you to walk, and your appointment is for ten o'clock Saturday morning."

"You're taking over my whole life, Anastasia Krupnik."

"No, I'm not. I'm just helping you get your life started. I'm sorry if it's rude to say this, Gertrustein, but I think your life ended when Mr. Stein — the man, not the goldfish — ran off with his mandolin player. And that was forty years ago!"

Gertrustein smiled suddenly. "You're right, Anastasia, but you're also wrong. My life ended when Edward Evans married the local nursery school teacher forty-seven years ago. Too late to start it up again now. But all right. I'll go and get a permanent at ten o'clock Saturday morning."

"Then you'll make new friends, and . . ."

"Hold on there. I will get a permanent. Then I will come home and feed my fish and watch TV. One thing at a time. I'm too old for any more changes."

"Good grief," said Anastasia suddenly. "I forgot something. Mom wanted you to babysit for Sam on Saturday. And it's really important. Maybe I should call and change that appointment . . ."

"No. Sam can come with me. I'll need the moral support."

The thought of someone who wears Pampers being moral support was a little startling to Anastasia, but it did seem to solve the problem.

And she was beginning to have another idea. Maybe it would be meddling in Gertrustein's life. On the other hand, she had *already* meddled in Gertrustein's life quite a bit, and it had seemed to work out okay. If *this* idea worked . . .

"I have to go someplace," she announced. "I'll see you later, Gertrustein."

She ran to the garage and wheeled out her bike.

*

Anastasia had already been to the small library. It was one of the first things she had done after they moved, finding the library and getting a library card.

In Cambridge, there had been a branch library not far from the Krupniks' apartment. Anastasia had been going to it since she was Sam's age: not by herself at that age, of course, but holding her mother's hand. Once, just before she moved, she had figured out that — if she had checked out eight books every week from the time she was two — she had taken more than four thousand books out of that library. That was a little puzzling, because the branch library was so small that she didn't think it *had* four thousand books. But her mother had pointed out that sometimes she took the same books over and over again.

In Cambridge, they knew her so well at the branch library that they called her Anastasia Again, the way Gertrustein was beginning to.

At this new library, they didn't know her at all, at least not *yet*, which was a little depressing. But they would. She had looked through their card catalogue and discovered they were missing some of her favorite books, so she was planning to write them a letter. One book that had been her favorite for years, in Cambridge, described all the symptoms of leprosy in great detail. She had checked it out regularly once every few months, just to be sure once again that she didn't have leprosy. Sometimes it was hard to tell, because one of the symptoms was itchy ear lobes. Every now and then Anastasia had itchy ear lobes. When she did, she always checked out the leprosy book so that she could read the other symptoms and be certain she didn't have them, too. Now that she lived in a town whose library didn't contain the leprosy book, she didn't know what she would do when her ear lobes itched. So she was going to mention that in her letter to the local library — politely, of course.

But right now she was headed, on her bike, for the building that she had noticed next door to the library. It was called the Senior Citizens Drop-in Center.

The door was open, and people looked up when she entered. It was probably pretty obvious, she realized, that she wasn't a Senior Citizen. Anastasia was not, in fact, a Senior Anything. She had dropped out of Girl Scouts as soon as she realized how awful she looked in a Girl Scout uniform, so she would never be a Senior Girl Scout. And she had given up on swimming lessons just after she passed Advanced Beginner, because it was such an effort not to sink. So she would never get her Senior Lifesaving badge.

Inside the door was a bulletin board, and Anastasia read announcements of painting classes, a trip to a flower show, a Great Books discussion group, lectures by a financial expert, and a course in gourmet cooking. There was also a notice of a lost cat named Boots, who was wearing a red flea collar; and there was a wedding announcement.

The people who had gotten married were named Ida and Harry, so Anastasia knew that they were Senior Citizens. No one young was named Ida or Harry.

Most of the people in the Senior Citizens Drop-in Center had gray hair, except for one woman whose hair was bright orange and one man who had no hair at all. Some of them were playing cards, although they stopped when Anastasia came in and looked over at her, still holding their cards. "I said 'Four spades,'" one woman said, but the others didn't answer her. Two men were playing Ping-Pong, and they stopped, too, and looked at Anastasia. They were all pretty friendly looking, but they seemed surprised to see her there.

A young woman came out of the back room, saw Anastasia, and smiled.

"Hi there. I'm Fran McCormick, the director. Can I help you? Are you looking for someone?"

Anastasia introduced herself, and Fran McCormick shook her hand.

"I have a friend," said Anastasia, "who is a Senior Citizen."

"Oh? What's her name? I know everybody pretty well," said Fran McCormick.

"Well, her name is Gertru . . . Gertrude Stein. But you wouldn't know her. She never goes out of her house except sometimes to take my little brother for a walk."

Everyone was listening. Even the card players had put their cards down, although the lady who had said "four spades" looked a little impatient. One of the Ping-Pong players suddenly hit the ball across the net, and it went past the other player, who wasn't paying attention. "Hah! Gotcha!" said the man who had hit the ball, smugly. Then he turned, too, to listen to Anastasia, and the little plastic ball rolled into a corner of the room.

Well. With so many people watching her now, Anastasia began to feel as if she was making a speech. She had never liked making speeches. When they had to give oral reports in school, she had never once gotten a grade better than a B-minus, because she became nervous and said "ah" too often.

"Well, ah, let me start over," she said, when she realized so many people were listening. "My friend Gertrude Stein lives next door to me, and she's a Senior Citizen. But she's lonely. She eats all by herself, so she only eats TV dinners, and except for me and my little brother, she doesn't have anyone to talk to, although she's *interesting* to talk to, and, ah, her goldfish is getting fat because she feeds him too much, and she does it just because it makes her feel good to feed somebody, even if it's only a goldfish . . ."

For a moment, Anastasia felt as if that had been a stupid thing to say. But then she noticed that the Senior Citizens were nodding, as if they understood. Probably some of them had goldfish, too.

"Well, why don't you send her down here to us?" asked the man who had hit the Ping-Pong ball.

"She wouldn't come. She'd be scared. Maybe it sounds stupid to be scared when you're all grown up, and even *old*, but . . ."

But they interrupted her, murmuring to each other and

nodding again. They all seemed to understand about being scared, even if you were old.

"...and she pretends she's not scared, by being grouchy," Anastasia went on. They all nodded again.

"Let's send her an invitation to the square dance!" called out one of the card players.

"She'd throw it away. She'd say 'junk mail,' and throw it away," Anastasia explained.

"What do you suggest that we could do for her?" asked Fran McCormick.

"Well, since you're called a Drop-in Center," began Anastasia, "I thought maybe some of you could drop in on her. I could give you the address. It's not very far away."

But they all began shaking their heads.

"Not uninvited," said a tiny white-haired lady wearing a pink pants suit. "Really, that just isn't done. I wouldn't want anyone to drop in on *me* unexpectedly!"

The others agreed. Anastasia was surprised. She *liked* having unexpected guests. But apparently the Senior Citizens disagreed.

She thought for a minute. "Well then, *here's* an idea. Why don't you drop in on *me?* I live right next door. And you wouldn't be unexpected, because I'm inviting you. I'll make Kool-Aid and everything. And then ..."

Some of them were beginning to nod their heads. "And then you invite *her* over!" said the man with no hair.

"Right! And you can all make friends with her!"

"I'd come," said the orange-haired woman.

"Me too," called out some others.

"When?" asked someone.

"Well," said Anastasia, "she's getting a permanent on Saturday morning. The first time she's been to a beauty parlor in maybe thirty years."

"Saturday afternoon, then!" announced the bald man. "How many people could make it Saturday afternoon?"

Hands shot up, and Fran McCormick counted. Fourteen.

Anastasia wrote down her address. A thought nudged itself into the back of her head.

"By any chance," she asked the Senior Citizens, "are any of you named Edward Evans?"

But no one was. No one had ever heard of Edward Evans. Well, that would have been asking too much.

✻

Pedaling home, Anastasia felt pretty good. She was sure her parents wouldn't mind. Her mother would help her make Kool-Aid. Her father would dream up some kind of entertainment, although she'd have to tell him tactfully not to conduct Verdi's Requiem for the Senior Citizens. But maybe he could read some of his poetry to them.

Then she thought of something and almost rode her bike into someone's shrubbery. Good grief. Saturday.

What on earth was she going to tell Robert and Jenny?

✻

Chapter 2 was not very long, Anastasia realized, reading it over. Only one sentence. But she liked the way it ended, with a mysterious reference to the young girl's

Past and her Future. It was important to be very subtle in a mystery novel, so that readers wouldn't know exactly what was happening too early in the book. It was one of the troubles with Nancy Drew books, that they weren't subtle enough. Agatha Christie, now: *those* were subtle. In Agatha Christie books, you never knew who was bad and who was good. That was important.

"Chapter 3," she wrote. "In her new life, the young girl began to meet new people. A tall tennis player with blue eyes. An old woman who looked like a witch. A mysterious band of people who held regular meetings, and who were stricken with astonishment when the young girl showed up unexpectedly at their hide-out one day.

"At the same time, people from her past were still on her trail. The young man with the puzzling briefcase had found out where she lived, and she received a message that he was on his way. He was bringing with him an Irish woman with a chipped tooth."

There. Now she had a whole cast of characters, and the reader would not know yet who were villains and who were heroes.

Anastasia didn't know yet, either; but she would worry about that later.

11

"No. Absolutely not. I won't, under any circumstances."
Anastasia's mother stood in her studio, with a paintbrush
behind one ear and her hands planted firmly on her hips.

Anastasia glowered. "Why *not?*"

"Because it's a lie, and I won't tell anyone a lie on your
behalf. And on top of that, it's the *stupidest* lie I've ever
heard."

Anastasia was astonished. She had thought it was a terrific idea. "What's so stupid? Look, all you have to do is
call Jenny, and sound very sad, and tell her that she and
Robert shouldn't come on Saturday because you just
found out that I have leprosy and I've had to go to a leper
colony very suddenly."

"That's ridiculous."

"Maybe it's not so ridiculous. Maybe I really do have leprosy, as a matter of fact. My ear lobes itch. They've been itching all afternoon. It's an early symptom."

"It's a symptom that you haven't washed your ears. With all that hair washing you've been doing lately, you'd think you'd remember to wash your ears."

"*Mom*. That's gross."

"Not as gross as lying to your friends. Why don't you want them to come, anyway?"

Anastasia groaned and flopped down in an old stuffed chair covered with painty rags. "Oh, it's complicated. I invited some other people over Saturday. Some new people I just met."

Her mother looked at her, smiled, took the paintbrush from behind her ear, and set it on the table. She sat down on the arm of the chair and stroked Anastasia's head.

"Oh, sweetie, I'm so glad. Dad and I haven't wanted to say anything, but we've been worried about your making friends. Except for Steve, you haven't really met any other kids yet. That's wonderful, that now you have, and I'm delighted that you've invited them over."

Good grief. Anastasia felt, suddenly, the way she had when Robert Giannini told her about his retarded cousin: as if suddenly, before you knew it, it was too late to explain.

"No kidding, Anastasia, I'm really thrilled. And Robert and Jenny will fit right in, I'm sure. Listen, we can have a cookout or something. How many people are coming over?"

"Fourteen."

"Goodness, that's a lot for a cookout! But I guess we could manage hot dogs. And I could make a big potato salad . . ."

"Mom, really, just Kool-Aid will be fine. I told them it would just be for Kool-Aid."

"Well, whatever you think. But you know, we've been talking about getting a badminton set. We could get it before Saturday, and then . . ."

Anastasia pictured the Senior Citizens playing badminton. She pictured the ambulance pulling up, to cart away the ones with broken hips and heart attacks. She groaned.

"Mom, you know what I'd really like best? I'd really like it best if you and Dad would go off to a movie or something, Saturday afternoon."

Her mother stopped stroking her hair. Anastasia could tell that her feelings were hurt.

"You mean that you don't want Dad and me to be here and meet your new friends? All of a sudden you're embarrassed to have us old people around?"

"Oh, Mom," she groaned, "it's not that. It's . . . Oh, for pete's sake, I need to think."

Anastasia pulled herself up out of the chair and started up to her room. In the hall, Sam was flicking a flashlight on and off. He'd been playing with it all day.

"Flash!" said Sam, shining the light at her and laughing.

"Knock it off, Sam," Anastasia muttered.

Sam's lower lip began to quiver as he decided whether or not to cry. Anastasia walked past him and headed up the stairs to her room. Her ear lobes really did itch. She began to wish that she really *did* have leprosy. Good-by, cruel world. Life was just too confusing.

"Flash! Flash!" called Sam after her, blinking his light.

Anastasia slammed her door and decided to stay in her tower for a long time. Like the rest of her life.

*

But the phone rang. Whenever you decide to lock yourself in a tower for the rest of your life, for pete's sake, the phone always rings.

Anastasia's mother called from the first floor. "Anastasia?"

"What? Is it for me?"

"Come down here a minute, would you? I want to talk to you."

Anastasia clumped down the stairs. On the second floor, Sam swooped out of his bedroom, yelled "Flash!" and blinked his light at her.

"Knock it off, Sam!"

Sam grinned and scooted off into a closet. She could see his flashlight blinking beneath the closed closet door.

"What do you want? Was the phone for me?" she asked her mother.

"Not really. But it was puzzling. It was someone named Fran McCormick . . ."

"Then it *was* for me!"

"Well, she said she didn't need to speak to you. She wanted to check with me to make sure that it was all right with me that all these people were coming over on Saturday. I must say, that was considerate of her. I can't remember that any of your *other* friends ever thought to ask my permission for anything."

"What did you tell her?"

"I told her sure. I told her we were planning to make a big batch of Kool-Aid. But, Anastasia . . ."

"What?"

"Then she said that if it wasn't too much trouble, could we please use artificially sweetened Kool-Aid. Because Edna and Morris and Ernest have diabetes. That seems strange, Anastasia. I remember there was a child in your third-grade class who was diabetic, but for three kids out of a batch of fourteen to have diabetes? Well, that seems very peculiar to me. Where did you meet these kids?"

Anastasia was tempted to burst out laughing and to tell her mother that the "kids" were all Senior Citizens and that Edna and Morris and Ernest were all in their seventies or eighties. But she was mad at her mother. She was mad at her for worrying about her ability to make friends, for pete's sake.

"They have a kind of club," said Anastasia airily. "I was walking past where their clubhouse is, and I just decided to stop in. They were all in there playing cards. So we got to talking, and I invited them over. I have a knack for making friends, you know," she added meaningfully.

"What do you mean, a kind of club? What do you mean, they were in there playing cards? Were they playing poker or something? Have you gotten yourself involved with some sort of *gang*, Anastasia Krupnik?"

Anastasia looked angrily at her mother. "I suppose you

could call it that. You could call it a 'gang' if you want to. I myself don't like to make that kind of stereotyped statement."

"Anastasia Krupnik, if those fourteen people arrive here Saturday on *motorcycles* . . ."

Now Anastasia almost *did* laugh. But she was still mad at her mother. She looked down her nose, which was not hard to do because of her height.

"I don't believe any of them will arrive by motorcycle," she said haughtily, and turned to go back upstairs.

Sam ambushed her on the landing.

"FLASH!"

"MOM!" Anastasia yelled. "*Why* is Sam blinding everybody with that blasted flashlight?"

"Sam, put your light away for now," said her mother. "He and Mrs. Stein have a plan," she explained to Anastasia. "They're going to flash lights at each other from their bedrooms after dark. Don't ask me why."

"Ask *me* why," grinned Sam.

"Why, dummy?"

"Because we're playing Flasher. Gertrustein used to play Flasher when she was a little girl, and she had a friend who lived right in this house."

"Yeah, I know about her friend. Edward Evans. Some friend. He grew up and married someone else, and now all she has is a goldfish."

Sam wasn't listening. He had unscrewed the end of his flashlight and was examining the batteries.

"Anyway, dummy, you know what a *real* flasher is?"

"What?"

"Some jerk of a man who goes out wearing nothing at all but a raincoat, and then he jumps out unexpectedly and opens up his raincoat at people."

"Oh," said Sam, with interest. "Does he say 'Flash'?"

"How should I know? I never saw one."

"Well, *I* say 'Flash,' " said Sam, losing interest. "I'm a flasher with a flashlight. FLASH!" He shone the light in Anastasia's eyes again and ran off when she made a half-hearted attempt to grab him.

Anastasia let him go and plodded back up to her bedroom to peel more wallpaper.

*

But the telephone rang again. This time it was for Anastasia. Her mother called her from downstairs. She could tell from her mother's voice that she was still mad. Well, that was okay. Anastasia was still mad, too.

"Is it the motorcycle gang? Did they ask for the gun moll?" Anastasia asked her mother sarcastically.

"It's Steve Harvey," said her mother coldly. "I should have told him you were out stealing hubcaps."

"Ha ha. Very funny." Anastasia took the phone and disappeared into a closet with it.

"Hi, Steve."

"Hi. Listen, my mom had an idea. She's been wanting to welcome your family to the neighborhood. So she thought maybe your family and mine could go together for a picnic on Saturday. Maybe to Sturbridge or someplace."

Oh, rats. Oh, *rats*. Anastasia had been dying to meet

Steve's family. His father was a sportscaster who actually knew a lot of famous athletes personally. His mother was a lawyer with the district attorney's office, and she had prosecuted an ax murderer once. And his older sister, who was home for a visit, was almost six feet tall, Steve said. She was a ballet dancer in New York. Her real name was Anne, but she went by the name Anya professionally. Anastasia thought that was the most terrific, wonderful thing she had ever heard.

Anastasia had once wanted to be a ballet dancer herself. She had taken lessons when she was nine and ten, but her feet never seemed to work right. One day she had tried to show her mother the dance she was practicing for a recital. She had twirled around on one toe, and her other leg knocked over a floor lamp, which hit the TV and bent the antenna; the antenna knocked a picture off the wall, and the picture hit a cup of coffee, which overturned on a book called *Treasures of the Louvre*. Anastasia grabbed for the book, but she tripped on a wrinkle in the rug and fell against the coffee table, breaking one of the table's legs and spraining her own ankle. She had to have X rays and to wear an Ace bandage for three weeks, and she had missed the dance recital and quit taking ballet lessons.

Her father had said, at the time, that she should be in the *Guinness Book of World Records* because she had done three hundred dollars worth of damage in twenty-seven seconds. But she had checked in the *Guinness Book of World Records* and found that a tornado in Hastings, Nebraska, had beaten that record in 1947.

Still, she was dying to meet Anne Harvey. She was dying to meet a female who was almost six feet tall and hadn't become a professional basketball player.

But instead, on Saturday, instead of going to Sturbridge with the remarkable Harvey family, Anastasia was going to be serving Kool-Aid to fourteen senior citizens, and to creepo Robert Giannini, and to traitor Jenny MacCauley, who had gone to see *Casablanca* without her.

She felt like having a tantrum, the way Sam did sometimes, kicking the floor and shrieking.

But twelve was too old for that; and anyway, she didn't want Steve Harvey to hear her kicking the floor and shrieking. Steve had already said, once, that she seemed very sophisticated for twelve.

She had explained, when he said that, that probably it was because she grew up in Cambridge, which was a more sophisticated place than the suburbs.

Steve had agreed. But then he had said something surprising. He had said that before he met Anastasia, he had thought everyone who lived in Cambridge was weird. He had thought that they were all intellectuals who sat around in the evenings drinking rose hip tea and playing recorders.

Anastasia had confessed that before she met *him*, she thought that everyone who lived in the suburbs was boring and preppy, that they all wore shirts with alligators and went to Bermuda for spring vacation.

Steve said that he'd never been to Bermuda in his life, and that he always ripped the alligators off his shirts.

Anastasia said that she hated rose hip tea more than anything in the world except liver.

It had been kind of nice to find out that they were wrong about each other, that they had — it now occurred to her — made premature assumptions.

So she certainly wasn't going to screech and kick the floor now, even though she sure felt like it.

Instead she said, "I'm really sorry, Steve, but we won't be able to on Saturday. I have a couple of friends from Cambridge coming out to visit that day, and there are some other people stopping by, too."

"Well, maybe some other time," Steve said cheerfully.

Sure, thought Anastasia glumly. She happened to know that his sister was going back to New York on Sunday, to start rehearsals for a new ballet. Probably with Nureyev, for pete's sake.

"My life is ruined, and it's all your fault," she muttered to her mother, who was in her studio again, painting different shades of blue onto a large canvas. She had a blue daub on her chin.

"Why *my* fault?" called her mother after her, as she headed back up the stairs.

Anastasia didn't really have an answer for that. Since Steve Harvey couldn't hear her, she gave a very unsophisticated answer.

"Because I didn't *ask* to be born!" she bellowed.

And her mother had a very unsophisticated answer to *that*. "Nyah nyah," she called, and stuck out her tongue.

*

"Who was the young man with the mysteriously blinking light?" wrote Anastasia, at the beginning of Chapter 4.

"And what role was the cruel, subversive woman with blue paint on her chin going to play in all of this?" she went on.

It didn't seem fair to leave out her father. So she continued Chapter 4 by writing, "The tall, bearded stranger sipped thoughtfully at a beer, with his eyes closed, listening to Mozart."

In an Agatha Christie book, Anastasia realized, there had always been at least one murder by Chapter 4.

So she wrote ominously, "Mozart was dead."

Anastasia woke up early on Saturday morning, and before she opened her eyes, she heard a sound that sounded like Frank Goldfish.

"Frank?" she said sleepily. "What are you doing? Cut it out. It's too early to be playing. Go back to sleep."

But the sound continued, and Anastasia woke up a little more, opened her eyes a tiny bit, and realized it was raining. High up here, in her tower room, wet tree leaves were blowing against her windows.

Anastasia grinned. Terrific. Robert and Jenny wouldn't be able to ride their bikes out here in the rain. Probably her dad would be willing to drive Gertrustein down to the beauty parlor. Maybe the Harveys wouldn't go to

Sturbridge, and maybe Anastasia could walk over and meet Anne, at least, before she went back to New York. And in the afternoon, all the Senior Citizens could come; Fran McCormick would bring them in the van that was painted with a gross name: Oldster Roadster.

She turned over, hugged her pillow, and went back to sleep.

But when she woke again, later, the rain had stopped.

❖

Downstairs, her mother was brushing Sam's hair.

"Sam's going with Mrs. Stein to the beauty parlor," she said, "so I thought he'd better look glamorous."

"Don't let them cut your hair, Sam," said Anastasia, buttering a piece of toast.

"Do my curls look pretty?" asked Sam anxiously.

Good grief. There was so much that Sam didn't know yet.

"Not pretty, Sam," Anastasia told him. "Handsome. Boys aren't supposed to look pretty, only handsome."

"Oh."

"You're not taking your flashlight, are you?"

"No, it's in its hiding place. Tonight we play Flasher."

Anastasia's mother looked out the window. "It looks as if it might rain again. The sky's pretty gray." She went to the closet, got Sam's little raincoat, and buttoned him into it. "There you are, old buddy. Your stroller's over at Mrs. Stein's. Have a nice time. And behave yourself."

They watched through the window as Sam trotted

across the yard and climbed the steps to Gertrustein's porch.

"Now. What's next? Kool-Aid." Anastasia's mother got the Kool-Aid out of the cupboard. "Might as well make it now, so Robert and Jenny can have some when they get here. Be sure to tell them to leave plenty for the Mafia."

"*Mom!*"

Her mother chuckled. "Okay, I'm sorry. I'm sure your new friends are actually very nice, Anastasia. I was just in a rotten mood yesterday. I've been working on a painting for a week now, and it just isn't going very well. You know how grouchy your father gets when he's writing a poem that doesn't seem to work? And he blames us, even though we've never even seen the poem?"

Anastasia laughed. "Yeah. I've been writing a novel for about three months now, myself. It took me 2½ months just to think of a title. And now the novel doesn't seem to have much connection to the title."

"Goodness. That would be a problem."

"Also, I'm having a hard time getting all the ingredients in."

"Ingredients?"

"Mmmmm. It's a mystery novel. I finally put in lots of mysterious characters. Then I remembered I needed a dead person. So I got that in, at the end of Chapter 4. But there's no sex yet."

"Sex? Are you sure you need sex in a mystery novel?"

Anastasia thought. Nancy Drew books had no sex.

Nancy's boyfriend was a little retarded that way, Anastasia thought. He was old enough to *drive*, for pete's sake, but he went on for book after book after book, without ever developing any interest in sex. But that was one reason that Nancy Drew books were boring.

Agatha Christie books had hints of love affairs, but nothing explicit. Anastasia wanted her mystery novel to be even more interesting than Agatha Christie's.

"Yes," she said. "I need some explicit sex. Maybe in Chapter 5."

"Stir."

"Stir my novel?"

"No, dummy. Stir the Kool-Aid."

They filled several old cider jugs. "There," said her mother. "We can add ice cubes when we serve it."

"Probably my gangland friends will sneak some vodka in, too."

"*Anastasia.* You're not serious, are you?"

Anastasia groaned. "No, Mom. I was only kidding."

*

Watching from the front window, Anastasia saw them as they came around the corner. She grinned. Actually, it would be fun to see Jenny again. She had missed Jenny. Probably, if the situation had been reversed, she would have gone to see *Casablanca* herself, she had to admit.

But she groaned when she saw Robert. Good old jerko Giannini. Right here, right here at her very corner, for pete's sake, he had stopped his bike and was consulting a map. Anastasia could see that Jenny was pointing to the house and yelling at him. But Robert was busily consulting his map, which he then folded very carefully and put back in his pocket. Typical of Robert to be able to fold a map. He was the only person Anastasia had ever met who could fold a map.

And he had his briefcase, of course. She could make out its rectangular outline, even though it was wrapped in something. Of course. Dark green plastic. Typical, that Robert had wrapped his briefcase in a trash bag so that it wouldn't get wet. Gross.

And his feet. What was wrong with his feet? Anastasia squinted, so that she could see them more clearly. Oh, no. She couldn't believe it. Sick. SICK.

Robert Giannini was wearing rubbers.

"Hi, Jenny!" Anastasia said, and made a special face at her which meant: look at Robert, wearing rubbers.

"Hi," said Jenny, and made a face back which meant: I know, it's the grossest thing I've ever seen.

"Well," said Robert Giannini, "we made it, Anastasia."

"I can see that, Robert. Come on in."

*

Robert and Jenny loved Anastasia's new house. It made her feel good, showing it to them and seeing it in a new way herself, as she did. She felt a little like a real estate dealer, opening doors and saying "This is the study" and "This is the studio where my mother paints" (although she closed that door again quickly, when she realized that her mother had been working on a nude).

Especially she liked taking them up to her tower room.

Even with the wallpaper partly peeled off, the room was exciting, set up high in the tops of the trees, with a view that stretched so far that they could see the tall Hancock Building in Boston in the distance.

Robert said, "You know, Anastasia, when you pull off these layers of wallpaper, you peel away a whole history of your room. Who lived in the house last?"

Anastasia shrugged. "Some doctor and his wife. They had five kids."

"Well, probably one of the kids lived up here, don't you think? So this top layer of paper belongs to that kid."

He pulled off a section of that paper near the window. "Now, look," he said. "Green, with flowers, under that. Wonder who lived here then."

"Maybe a young couple," said Jenny. "Maybe the husband beat the wife, so she used to come up here to hide from him."

"That's really old-fashioned paper," said Anastasia, looking at the pattern more closely. "Probably it was way back in the 1930s or something, when everything was different. Maybe the wife wanted to go out and get a job instead of staying home and cooking. That's why he beat her."

"The rat," muttered Jenny.

"What's underneath?"

Robert picked with his fingernail at the green flowered paper until a piece of it came loose. "Blue. With a sort of striped pattern. This one's *really* old." He pulled more of the green away. "Wonder who lived here then."

"A family that had a crazy uncle. They kept him

chained up here in the tower," suggested Jenny.

"Yeah," said Robert. "He used to keep track of the days and weeks by making marks on the wall. Look! Right here is a mark he made!"

Robert was right. At the edge, still partly covered by the green paper, was a mark made with pen and ink.

"It probably says 'Help! I'm being held captive in this tower!' "

"Be careful, Robert. Don't tear it!"

Anastasia laughed after she said that. Telling someone who wears rubbers, carries a briefcase, and folds maps correctly to be careful. Really dumb.

He finally lifted up a strip of green paper and exposed all of the faded writing. They leaned over and tried to figure out what it said. It was certainly not the marks of a madman counting the days of captivity.

Anastasia made it out and opened her mouth in astonishment. "I know what that is! Good grief! Wait till . . ."

But she was interrupted. Her mother called from the bottom of the tower stairs.

"Anastasia! You get down here *right away!* Two vans just pulled into the driveway. Your guests are here!"

*

An hour later, some of the confusion had subsided. Everyone was on their second cup of Kool-Aid, and Anastasia's mother had opened the box of imported cookies that she'd been saving since last Christmas for a special occasion (although Edna, Morris, and Ernest, being diabetic, couldn't eat them).

Anastasia's father was in the study, showing off his first editions to Harry, who had once taught European literature at Tufts University, and to Jeanette, who years ago had managed a Boston book store.

Robert had opened his briefcase and was showing some rocket plans to Morris and Fred, who were retired engineers, and they were arguing over whether the rocket Robert had designed could possibly make it to the moon.

Edna and four other ladies were showing Jenny photographs of their grandchildren.

Someone was playing "Alexander's Ragtime Band" on the piano, and a tiny lady with snow-white hair was dancing around and around the dining room all by herself.

In the studio, the man with no hair at all was looking wistfully at the half-finished painting of a nude.

Someone kept asking if the Krupniks had a croquet set. Or a badminton set. Or a volleyball.

In the kitchen, Fran McCormick was helping Anastasia's mother make some more Kool-Aid, and they were both laughing so hard they were almost crying.

". . . and I thought she meant a motorcycle gang," Anastasia's mother sputtered. Anastasia wandered into the kitchen.

"Anastasia," laughed Fran, "I think your mother is going to clobber you after we leave."

Anastasia perched on a kitchen stool, chewed on a cookie, and grinned. "This is a good party," she said. "Even Robert Giannini is a hit. I think Robert is really an eighty-year-old man in a twelve-year-old body."

"Is everybody okay in there? The new batch of Kool-Aid's almost ready," said her mother, stirring.

"Everyone's fine. Someone wants to play croquet. Some other people are having a contest over who has the best-looking grandchildren, so there are photographs all over the place. The guy with the bald head wishes you had painted the breasts bigger on the nude."

"Tell him to go buy a *Playboy*."

"I did. And Mom, I just saw Gertrustein and Sam go into her house. The point of this party was to introduce Gertrustein to everyone. How shall we get her to come over?"

Her mother went to the telephone and dialed.

"Mrs. Stein? This is Katherine Krupnik. How did it go at the beauty parlor?"

"Don't tell her there are *people* here," hissed Anastasia, "or she won't come." Her mother gestured to her to be quiet.

"Oh, Gertrude, I'm sure it looks *lovely*. You just aren't used to it."

Anastasia remembered something. "Tell her," she whispered, "that I have something I absolutely *have* to show her."

Her mother gestured: Shut up.

"Of course you're not going to wear a hat for the rest of your life," her mother was saying into the phone. "He *what*? That little beast!"

She put her hand over the receiver and whispered to Fran and Anastasia, "Sam told her she looks like Art Garfunkel."

"Sam *loves* Art Garfunkel," said Anastasia.

"Gertrude, Anastasia tells me that Sam loves Art Garfunkel," her mother said into the telephone. "So he means it as a compliment. Listen, Gertrude, why don't you bring Sam over here now? I want to see your permanent, and Anastasia has something that she says she absolutely has to show you."

After she hung up, she said apprehensively to Fran and Anastasia, "This may be a terrible mistake. She says she intends to put on a large hat and go to bed in a dark room for the rest of her life."

"*Mom*," Anastasia pointed out, "she's saying that for the same reason she says she doesn't like people. She's *scared*. Is she coming over?"

"Yes. In fact, there she is now, coming out of her house with Sam. You go and greet her at the door, Anastasia."

They watched through the window as Gertrustein and Sam came across the yard, and Anastasia ran to open the door.

Gertrustein was, as she had said, wearing a large green hat which covered her hair.

"Good afternoon, Anastasia," she said. "I've brought your brother back. And your mother says you have something to show me."

The piano began again, with "You Are My Sunshine." People began to sing. There was a thump in the dining room, and Anastasia cringed; the white-haired lady had bumped into the table as she danced.

Sam looked startled at the noise. He dropped Gertru-

138

stein's hand, said, "I'm going to hide," and scooted up the stairs.

"I wasn't aware that you had guests," Gertrustein sniffed. "I'll come back another time."

"No, no, it's okay," said Anastasia casually. "It's just some friends who stopped by. Come on in." She took Gertrustein by the hand and practically dragged her into the living room.

"Everybody," announced Anastasia in a loud voice, "I would like you to meet my friend Gertrude Stein."

The Senior Citizens clustered around Gertrustein, introducing themselves. Someone put a paper cup of Kool-Aid into her hand. The woman with orange hair sat back down at the piano and began to play "As Time Goes By," the song from *Casablanca*. "A kiss is just a kiss . . ." Edna and Fred began to sing.

"Here's lookin' at you, kid," said the bald-headed man in a not-too-bad Humphrey Bogart voice to Gertrustein, and held up his cup of Kool-Aid in a toast.

Anastasia saw that Gertrustein's mouth was beginning to twitch at the edges into a smile.

The doorbell rang.

At the door was Steve Harvey, with the tallest, most beautiful girl Anastasia had ever seen.

"I didn't realize you were having so much company," Steve said loudly to make himself heard over the noise. "This is Anne. We didn't go to Sturbridge because of the rain this morning, and Anne wanted to meet you before she goes back to New York."

Anastasia grinned, shook Anne's hand, and brought them inside. She thought for a minute that she would try to explain about the company. Then she looked in the living room, saw seven Senior Citizens, plus Gertrustein still wearing her big green hat, arranging themselves into a circle to do some sort of dance, and decided that it would be impossible to explain.

"My parents are outside in the car," explained Steve. "Do you think . . ."

"Sure," said Anastasia. "Bring them in."

*

Finally, the noise had lessened. Everyone was worn out, and the Kool-Aid was almost gone. Anne Harvey had demonstrated a dance from a Broadway musical, and when she had asked politely if she could wear Gertrustein's green hat for the dance, Gertrustein had finally taken the hat off. Everyone had admired her new mass of silver curls. There had been a long discussion about Art Garfunkel, and they had played an Art Garfunkel record on the stereo.

Mr. Harvey had done an imitation of Howard Cosell. Anastasia's father had read a poem about baseball. Then Mr. Harvey had read the same poem in his Howard Cosell voice.

The man with the bald head was now wearing the big green hat.

Everyone was exhausted from laughing and singing. For the first time in two hours, the house was quiet, as they all gathered their breath in order to say good-by.

There was the soft padding sound of bare feet coming down the stairs.

"It's my brother," said Anastasia softly. "I wondered what had happened to him."

Sam appeared in the doorway, and everyone said, "Oooooh," the way people do when they see a curly-headed baby.

But Anastasia's heart sank. No, Sam, she said silently. Don't do it, Sam. She cringed. The instant she saw that Sam was wearing his raincoat and that below it his legs and feet were bare, she knew what was coming. I'll kill you, Sam, she thought.

Sam grinned and stood in the doorway looking at the room full of senior citizens, and Gertrustein, and his parents, and the Harveys, and Jenny, and Robert.

"FLASH!" he said loudly and opened his raincoat. Then he scampered away, naked.

Everyone sat politely silent for a moment. Then the Senior Citizens began to giggle. Anne Harvey started to laugh. Gertrustein laughed so hard that her Art Garfunkel curls shook. Mr. Harvey announced, "Ladies and gentlemen, an astonishing thing has happened," in his Howard Cosell voice.

It was time for everyone to go home.

※

"Gertrustein, I really do like your hair," said Anastasia, "and I'm glad you had fun at the party."

"Hmmmph," said Gertrustein.

Sam had been tucked away for his nap, and they were cleaning up the kitchen.

"Mom, do you know what Robert Giannini said, when he and Jenny were leaving?"

"What?"

Anastasia giggled. "He came over to me privately and said in this very serious voice, 'Anastasia, I thought that your brother had a birth defect. I didn't realize that you meant he was emotionally disturbed. I'm really sorry.'"

"That jerk," said Anastasia's mother. "Of course, Sam really was obnoxious, I'll admit."

"It was probably my fault," pointed out Gertrustein, "since it was I who suggested to him that we play Flasher."

"Gertrustein!" said Anastasia. "I just remembered! I really *do* have something to show you! Do you think you could climb up all the stairs to my room?"

Gertrustein groaned. "Can't you bring it down?"

"No. Come on. We can go slow."

The two of them climbed the staircase to the second floor; then, puffing, Gertrustein made it up to the tower.

"Actually," she said, "I think the dancing helped my arthritis. I think maybe I'll enroll in their folk-dancing class."

"Look!" said Anastasia. "Kneel down here, Gertrustein, so you can see."

They knelt side by side, and Anastasia pointed to the faded writing on the oldest layer of wallpaper.

"'Edward loves Gertrude. Always,'" Gertrustein read

aloud. "My goodness. I wonder when he wrote that."

"There's no date."

"Well, it really doesn't matter when he wrote it, I guess. It's nice to know that he *did*." Gertrustein blushed a little.

"I wonder where he is now."

"Probably being a Senior Citizen somewhere."

"Maybe you could find him."

But Gertrustein hooted. "I wouldn't even want to, now. He's probably fat. Better just to remember him. Of course, it would be nice if . . ."

"If what?"

Gertrustein patted her curls. "If he could see my new hairdo," she laughed.

✻

"Chapter 5," wrote Anastasia at the top of a new page. She had begun to be a little bored with novel writing, so she decided that Chapter 5 would be the final chapter. That meant, she knew from Agatha Christie, that she had to bring all the characters together, preferably in a locked room, and solve the mystery.

And she also had to put the sex in.

She realized that it was not entirely clear just what the mystery *was*. But it was in the title. "The Mystery of Saying Good-by." Okay. She just had to connect the title with the plot.

Anastasia spit out some eraser bits that she had nibbled off accidentally and began to write.

"All of the characters," she wrote, "were in the same

room. Suddenly, creeping silently down from the tower, came a naked man."

Then she frowned, crossed out "man" and wrote "little boy."

But that was no good. There was nothing at all sexy about a little boy, naked or not. Well, she thought, it *is* a novel. It doesn't have to be exactly true.

So she wrote again, "Suddenly, creeping silently down from the tower, came a naked man. All he was wearing was a trench coat, and he carried a flashlight.

"He threw open the door to the room, opened his trench coat, laughed an evil laugh, and disappeared."

There. So much for the sex. Now to connect the title.

"The tall bearded man said to everyone, 'Good-by. I am going to take a nap now.'

"The blue-eyed tennis player said to the young girl, 'Good-by. Do you want to play tennis later if it doesn't rain?'

"The young girl said, 'Good-by. Yes, I do.'

"The tall ballerina said, 'Good-by. I think I will go to New York now, to be in a ballet.'

"The cruel and subversive housewife, who actually turned out to be pretty nice, said, 'Good-by. I am going to wash the Kool-Aid pitchers.'

"The woman who looked like a witch, except she didn't anymore, said, 'Good-by. I will help you wash the Kool-Aid pitchers. Where is my green hat?'

"The bald man who was wearing her green hat took it off and gave it to her. 'Good-by,' he said. 'Maybe we could have dinner together some night soon.'

"A whole batch of old people said, 'Good-by,' and they went home. Some of them had to babysit for their grand-children.

"The strange young man wearing a SeaWorld tee shirt said, 'Good-by, everyone. I am sorry about the naked, emotionally disturbed man. Where is my briefcase?'

"The Irishwoman with the chipped tooth said, 'Here it is. Don't forget your dumb rubbers. Good-by, all.'

"The famous sportscaster said, 'This is Howard Cosell wishing you good-by after what has proven to be an eventful afternoon.'

"The lady lawyer who had once prosecuted an ax mur-derer said, 'Will you stop that ridiculous Howard Cosell imitation! Good-by, everyone. Thank you so much for including us.'

"The young girl realized, after they had all left, that there were many different ways to say good-by. That solved the mystery."

Anastasia read Chapter 5 again. It was the longest chapter of her novel. But she realized it was lacking something still.

Two things, she decided. The sex was not *quite* ex-plicit enough. And there should have been another men-tion of the corpse.

But those things were easy to add. She wrote two more sentences.

"The naked man had a poking-out bellybutton. And Mozart was still dead."

Then she wrote, "The End" and went to get her tennis racket.